Rourke stood. "There," he shouted. "No weapons!"

He stepped back one step, then a second one, then a third. His palms sweated.

There were boulder-sized rocks scattered all along the top of the mountain and from behind one of these now stepped a man. He was clad in human skins, a woman's head of hair dangling obscenely near his crotch. In his right hand was a stone axe—the handle perhaps two feet long, a massive flat rock laced to it with what Rourke surmised would likely be human hair woven into rope. "Do you speak English?" Rourke called out.

The cannibal's face seamed with something halfway between a smile and a snarl, his body bending slightly forward as his left hand joined his right on the axe. From behind another rock came another of the cannibals. Then from behind still another rock still a third, the second two armed like the first, each with a massive stone axe.

Rourke didn't move away. "I didn't come to kill you. I want my son!"

The first cannibal kept coming, raising the stone axe now to swing. . . .

THE SURVIVALIST

#10

THE AWAKENING

BY JERRY AHERN

ZEBRA BOOKS
KENSINGTON PUBLISHING CORP.

ZEBRA BOOKS

are published by

Kensington Publishing Corp.
475 Park Avenue South
New York, N.Y. 10016

Third printing: September 1986

Printed in the United States of America

For my readers—thank you. . . .

Chapter One

It was another dream, another in the endless succession of dreams, of nightmare fantasy and reality, of happiness and pleasure—another of the dreams. He had long since become aware of them, viewing them from the peculiar position of observer yet at once participant. He had even learned to control them. When a scene in the dream would be violent, when he was against insurmountable odds, he would stop the dream, go back several scenes and provide an additional weapon for himself, extra explosives, some added means of escape. He tried that when he came upon an electrified fence—like the one that had surrounded the Womb—and for some reason despite his precautions, the electrified fence was sending a charge through his body. The funny thing of it was that the charge was not killing him—but did one ever die in dreams, he wondered? In fact, the charge was almost pleasant. He felt the tingling sensation in his body—as if it were somehow animating him rather than destroying him.

He considered this, in the surreal way in which dreamers can consider anything—why was it pleasant?

Enough of this dream.

He opened his eyes.

John Rourke opened his eyes.

He could breathe.

He closed his eyes—but he realized at one level of consciousness that it was not a dream now. He was at last awake.

John Rourke realized he was alive.

To sit up was impossible yet—he felt only the tickle of the electrical charge, the sensation of light touching his eyes, his eyes unused for five centuries. The sensation of the rising and falling of his chest.

There was no danger of falling asleep.

But with his eyes closed, he felt his body awakening, never more aware of his body in so physical a way—it was like orgasm, only with the entire body as its focal point.

Alive . . .

Rourke sat up, the lid of the cryogenic chamber rising in rhythm with his body.

He turned his head—he had been practicing that. The monitoring lights still glowed on the five other cryogenic chambers, still sealed. They too were alive—Sarah, Michael, Annie, Paul—and his eyes rested on Natalia. He closed his eyes. She was beautiful even in her sleep as the swirling

8

clouds of the bluish gas drifted across her face. But he missed the surreal blue of her eyes.

John Rourke looked to his right.

His Rolex Submariner—he picked it up and as he did the sweep second hand started to move again. He would have to ascertain the correct time, the correct date. Slowly—not moving well yet—he placed the watch on his wrist and closed the flip-lock clasp in place to secure it there. Beside the watch—the twin stainless Detonics .45s.

He remembered now.

There had been the fight with the last Soviet helicopter. He had killed Rozhdestvenskiy and Rozhdestvenskiy's submachine gun—it was an Uzi, Rourke recalled for some strange reason—had fired into the chopper. The chopper had exploded and Rourke had dived for the escape tunnel. He remembered a wound to his left forearm, a rock chip. He had cleaned the wound, dressed it while he had gone about the rest of his business in preparing the Retreat.

The world had been dying outside.

He had removed the bandage just before entering his chamber, just before injecting himself with the cryogenic serum.

The hypodermic needle—it lay on the floor beside the chamber now as he looked down. And he looked at his arm. The wound was healed and there was no scar.

His pistols. Rourke had cleaned them, leaving them unloaded. He picked up one of the pistols— the lubrication was still in evidence.

9

He was naked from the waist up, and bootless and sockless.

Slowly, he began to move his legs. . . .

Rourke's feet were over the side now, the pair of rubber thongs beside the chamber, the thongs that he had worn while cleaning the guns, securing the Retreat. He remembered that. He placed his feet in them and tried to stand—slowly.

He could stand, but he leaned against the cryogenic chamber for support.

He started to walk, the twin Detonics Combat Masters in the hip pockets of his beltless Levi's— his pants felt a little large on him at the waist. Weight loss, he supposed, the body burning energy however minutely for higher brain functions and the like.

There was a mirror in the bathroom—he started toward it, not having to urinate yet, but knowing that he should try to get his body working again. Water.

He was suddenly cotton-mouthed, thirsty. He continued toward the bathroom, up the three low steps, the steps hard going, hard to balance on, but he reached the bathroom.

Rourke activated the electrical pump for the water system, hearing it come on, turning on the cold water—air sputtered through the pipe, making loud noises, then a trickle of water from the tap, a murky yellow color, more air, a bubble of gas, then water, clean looking.

He let it run for a time, looking up to see himself in the mirror.

His hair was a little longer than he remembered it. He could cut it himself. He had taught himself to do that. He had a beard that looked the equivalent of two weeks or so of growth—he'd grown beards before, sometimes involuntarily in the field. His eyes were clear. Wrinkles that had been at their corners were now gone.

The scar on the base of his left ear lobe where a bullet had nicked him—the scar was gone.

He had suspected the cryogenic process might serve to restore and rejuvenate the body, from the data he had seen. He felt, somehow, younger.

Rourke sat down on the toilet, the lid down, to rest while the water ran. . . .

He had drunk water after first testing it for purity—it was as pure as it had been. The underground stream had not failed him.

He had cooked a meal of cream of wheat and lightly toasted whole wheat bread. He had one cup of black coffee—he had barely made it to the bathroom in time, but the results had been normal, healthy.

In the area beyond the confines of the living section of the Retreat he had constructed a ballistic test chamber. With boxes of ammunition selected at random and the twin Detonics pistols—he wore a shirt now and a belt, the belt notched in tight against his newer thinness—he went to this section of the Retreat. The primary generators hummed, working perfectly. He would detail-inspect them later.

But defense—it might be important.

Four boxes of Federal 185-grain JHP .45s. He selected one round from each box, having first more closely inspected his guns, removing excess lubrication.

He fired the four rounds into the test chamber, the chronograph reading showing the proper muzzle velocity, the functioning of guns and ammunition combined as perfect as ever.

He loaded the magazines for both pistols, reinserting them, working the slides, lowering the hammers over the live rounds. He loaded the half-dozen magazines from the black leather Milt Sparks Six Pack, the Six Pack already on his belt.

Rourke inserted the Detonics pistols into the double Alessi shoulder rig, settling the holsters on his body—the familiarity of the weight.

He returned to the main portion of the Retreat—his little A. G. Russell Sting IA black chrome—he positioned this inside his trouser band behind his left hip bone. And the bone was easier to find with the loss of weight.

Socks and boots. There would be time for a shower later.

He found boot socks, pulled them on, then a pair of combat boots. He pulled these on, lacing them up.

His bomber jacket—before putting himself to sleep he had saddle soaped it. He pulled it on now, his gloves in the side pocket—they were still soft, supple. He pulled on the gloves.

Not a cigar—not yet.

His dark-lensed aviator-style sunglasses—he

placed these in the inside pocket of his coat.

He had no idea if it was day or night outside. He had been awake for nearly five hours.

He checked the charge for the battery units for one of the Geiger counters. Adequate.

John Rourke started for the escape tunnel.

It had a double hermetic seal.

It was the only way to know. . . .

His muscles were unused to working—and he was tired as he climbed the rungs of the tunnel from the interior door, a rechargeable flashlight in his jacket, the light swaying as he moved.

The barred hermetically sealed door. He opened this—cold.

The air seemed somehow thinner to him. But he could breathe it. He had tested the Geiger counter against the luminous face of the Rolex. But it read nothing now. He checked it against the watch face again—the radiation detector worked. But there was no high level of background radiation.

Rourke climbed through the tunnel, securing the hermetically sealed door behind him. He kept climbing upward, toward the final door.

Did a viable world lay above it?

He worked away the bar. The rubber gasket still had its integrity but the rubber was a little dry—he made a mental note to lubricate it. He used the Geiger counter again with the door only open a small crack so he could close it quickly.

No alarming level of background radiation.

He opened the door, turning his face away, putting on the glasses. There was no way to test for

13

ozone content. Skin cancer was a risk he would endure—but the signs of excessive incoming solar radiation would show up quickly.

He moved through the last door into the blinding sunlight. Squinting against it, despite the dark-lensed glasses, he climbed out, exhausted from the climb, muscle weary, his breathing labored—the air was rarer than it had been but that was to be expected.

The digital readout on the cryogenic chamber had shown 481 years to have passed.

He stood up—around him was desert, at the base of the mountain and beyond.

Binoculars—he took the Bushnells from their case at his side. Shivering again against the cold, he estimated the ambient temperature in the fifties and it was midday.

He focused the Bushnell eight-by-thirtys—in the far distance, there was green, patches of it, like sparse grass.

John Rourke dropped to his knees—half from exhaustion and half from a more compelling necessity.

He made the sign of the cross.

Chapter Two

Still using the escape tunnel and keeping

the main entrance sealed, Rourke sortied into the world often throughout the next several days, testing the atmosphere against his own skin. After six days, he determined that although prolonged exposure to the sun would have its effects because of the thinness of the atmosphere, a sufficient amount of the ozone layer had survived and/or been restored so that with some care it would not be lethal to be out of doors. He determined this as best he could—only long-term time would truly tell, perhaps fatally.

But life in itself was a gamble.

Judging from the exact readout on the chamber in terms of years and decimal values thereof—and from readings on the position of the sun and some of the more regular constellations in the brilliant night sky (there was less distortion now because of the thinner atmosphere)—he calculated the date of his awakening as September twelfth, and the year as well.

He was also able to set his watch precisely, as well as the electric clocks throughout the Retreat.

Time was now a definitive commodity, measuring, rather than merely elapsed time, an orderly progression.

One by one, he had checked the systems within the Retreat—a minor repair here, an alteration there.

He experimented with the food. It had survived, the meat irradiated to kill bacteria before storage proving now exceedingly worthwhile.

He was on solid foods, his appetite coming back

to him, his bodily functions normal.

A complete physical—as complete as a physician can give himself. His heart rate was better than it had been since his early twenties. So was his pulse. His hearing was better, too.

Smoking no longer a habit, he consumed three cigars a day or less. He calculated that, at that rate, he had enough for three years, perhaps a little longer. He had prepared. Tobacco could be grown.

He had begun a program of rigorous physical activity, large muscle group function to strengthen the heart and to tone the body and develop lung power.

At midday on the sixth day he used a soil test kit to determine the viability of the land near the Retreat, for the first time using the main entrance.

The soil was richer than it had ever been, despite the sandy appearance. It was bleached by the stronger sun. He was tanning rapidly and by the fifth day had begun to wear one of his broad-brimmed Stetsons against the sun.

Beneath the topsoil, the ground was still dark and rich. Some nutrients were in bizarre combinations—but it would grow food.

He had tested all of his weapons and ammunition—all was in order.

Gradually, he was recharging the battery for the Harley Low Rider.

But he was alone.

Chapter Three

On the seventh day, September eighteenth, he did not rest.

He was not God and so there was no special reason, for dramatic meaning or otherwise, to do so.

His plan was one he had considered carefully, one in which he had no choice but to place his confidence. For the survival of them all, it was necessity.

He stood—one of his cigars, the first of the day, was clamped tightly in the left side of his mouth between his teeth, unlit. Rourke stared at the cryogenic chambers.

His hair was cut. He could feel his muscle power returning more rapidly than he had anticipated. He was clean shaven and had a full stomach.

Alive in all but the fullest sense of the word.

He activated the controls of the cryogenic chambers, to awaken his son and his daughter.

He sat down on the sofa which had been pushed aside to make room for the cryogenic chambers when they had first been brought to the Retreat, watching the slow awakening process begin—the gas began to swirl in different patterns, to slowly dissipate.

He watched. . . .

John Rourke was fascinated—the process took hours. He felt overly clinical, but he made notes as he watched, smiling too as expression returned to the face of his young daughter, to the face of his young son.

Annie's hair had grown—perhaps two inches. Michael's hair had grown as well—he could give Michael a haircut. The longer length hair looked pleasing on Annie.

Rourke watched them turn their heads, evidently passing through the state where dreams and returning consciousness co-mingled, as he had—it fascinated him how long this process seemed to endure. And he wondered what children's dreams were. His dreams in childhood had long since faded in his memory.

Rourke watched. He noted things in the legal pad before him.

He remembered things in his heart—he wondered how it would be to watch his wife Sarah, Natalia, Paul. How would it be for them?

To awaken.

Annie began to sit up. Michael—always the harder of the two children to awaken—still moved, but in a supine position, tossing, turning.

The lid of Annie's chamber began to rise, coordinated with the rising of her seven-year-old body. That she had been born 488 years ago did not escape him—the irony of it.

The cryogenic chamber's lid was fully open.

"Hello, sweetheart," Rourke whispered—for the first time since his awakening having someone with whom to speak.

"Da—"

Her mouth wasn't working properly yet and he

laughed, standing up, walking over to stand beside the chamber, reaching out his right hand to hold her hands. "We're all alive. We made it. You've been sleeping for four hundred and eighty-one years."

"How—how—"

"How long is that? It's a very long time, longer than any other human being has ever slept and then awakened. The people on the Eden Project—they've been sleeping a little longer, but they're still asleep. They should be for another twenty-one years. Do you understand me?"

Annie yawned, like only a little girl yawns, her body scrunching up, her mouth open, her arms outstretching.

And she smiled—he had remembered how beautiful her smile was, at least he had thought he had. But seeing it now was even more than he had remembered. He noticed too that the small chicken pox scar that had been on her eyelid, and the mark on her hand from the removal of a wart—both scars were gone now.

She hugged her arms—awkwardly—around his neck. He lifted her from the chamber, kissing her cheek.

In the cryogenic chamber to the right, Rourke's left, Michael was beginning to move with greater determination it seemed—and he was starting to rise, the lid of the chamber rising, the slightly sweet smell of the cryogenic gas again as it dissipated.

Michael sat fully erect.

19

"Hi, son."

Michael looked at him oddly. And then it looked like Michael was starting to laugh.

Chapter Four

Oddly, the children had seemed tired after only a few hours of wakefulness—but a rapid yet complete examination had revealed no unexpected physical conditions, no illness. They were simply children—something which Rourke had consciously reminded himself to remember—and been exhausted by the excitement.

After eight hours of sleep, a surprisingly large breakfast and endless questions about the cryogenic process, Rourke stood with them before the open outer door of the Retreat. It was their first sight of the New World.

"It looks like a desert," Annie observed. "But it's kinda pretty, isn't it, Daddy?"

"Yes—kind of pretty," Rourke answered, smoking his first cigar of the day. "Kind of."

"Is everything dead out there?" Michael asked suddenly, his shoulders hunched in the too large blue denim jacket Rourke had loaned him.

Rourke didn't answer for a moment.

Annie repeated Michael's question. "Is it all dead out there?"

"I thought that it would be—and in a way it is. But I was awake for a week before I awakened you, Annie, or you, Michael. And I did a lot of thinking." He started through the outer doorway —the rocks were still in place as they should be, the rocks which he used as the counterbalances for opening the door of the Retreat. He perched on a rock near them, Annie squirming up onto his lap, Michael leaning on his shoulder at his left. Rourke carried his Detonics pistols only. "There might have been other nations which foresaw what could happen and prepared, maybe other groups. There were a lot of Survivalists in the days before the Night of The War. If an elaborate enough Retreat could have been built, one that was self-sustaining —well, maybe we aren't alone." And he smiled, hugging Annie tighter on his lap, holding Michael close, too. "But we're alone here—as far as the eye can see, even with binoculars." He pointed toward the top of the mountain. "From way up there, I can see vegetation—plants, you know. But no signs of fish in the streams, animal life—or people. No campfires, no smokestacks, no vehicles —like the land around us was wiped clean like a chalkboard and no one has written on it yet. And that's what I want to talk to you both about." The air temperature was chill, but Rourke felt a warmth in him he rarely felt as he held his children. "The Eden Project—"

"The spaceships," Annie supplied.

"Space Shuttles," Michael corrected, seemingly automatically.

"Shuttles, ships—but the Eden Project. They should return in about twenty-one years if the data was correct. But what if the Eden Project never returned, and what if we were the only people on Earth?"

"I wouldn't have anybody to play with," Annie said softly.

Rourke smiled, holding her. "More important that that—and I know playing is important—but more important than that even: survival, not just of ourselves, but the human race. The three of us here, and your mother, and Uncle Paul and Natalia—only six people. I thought a long time about this. Our chances of rebuilding, of making a new world—the only way is for all six of us to be adults at the same time, for all six of us to be as close in age as possible. And so I have a plan. You'd both have to be very brave and be very smart."

"What is it that you want us to do, Daddy?"

He looked at his son's lean face, the brown eyes, the full shock of dark brown hair—it was as if somehow he were studying his own reflection in a mirror, but the light bringing him the reflection had taken a quarter century to return from the mirror to his eyes. "For the next five years, I'm going to teach both of you everything, some things you probably shouldn't know until you are much older. We're going to work very hard—"

"Will we have a chance to play, Daddy?" Annie smiled.

"Yes—there'll be time for that, too."

"Why five years?" Michael asked him.

"Because, son, in five years you'll be nearly fourteen biologically," and he looked at Annie on his lap, her dark honey blond hair caught up in the breeze, her brown eyes sparkling. "And you, young lady—you'll be nearly twelve. That's awfully young for both of you—"

"Fourteen is pretty old," Michael insisted.

Rourke let himself smile. "It's going to have to be. Because in five years, if everything goes as I plan, I'm taking the cryogenic sleep again. For sixteen years. And when you are thirty, Michael—and Annie, you'll be twenty-eight. Then all the chambers will open, your mother's, Paul's, Natalia's—and mine again." He looked at his son. "You'll be about two years older than Natalia, Michael." He looked at Annie. "And you'll be just a little younger than Paul Rubenstein. And Mommy and Daddy won't be that much older than either of you. Then there'll be six of us—and we can build the world again if we have to."

They didn't understand, Rourke thought. His children didn't understand.

But in Michael's eyes, he saw something. Rourke knew that he would.

"Our first lesson in survival and in growing up begins today. So run—don't run far, but run and play."

Annie kissed him on the lips and slipped off his lap, running after Michael. Rourke watched as they played tag down the mountain road from the entrance of the Retreat. "Play," John Rourke

23

whispered. "While you can." He inhaled on his cigar but it had gone dead. He lit it again in the blue-yellow flame of his Zippo.

Chapter Five

The most important task at the beginning had been teaching Annie to do more than just pretend to read. And she had learned quickly. And he had immediately begun each child in the ways of self-preservation. Michael had been taught the rudiments of marskmanship before the Night of The War. And from what Sarah had told him, Michael had learned these rudiments well. He found himself—John Rourke—sometimes watching Michael in those first days. Nine years old and the boy had already killed. But it seemed not to affect him.

The subject matter to be taught and mastered had been overwhelming, Rourke had realized from the start. Electronics, plumbing, electrical work, motorcycle maintenance—all these to preserve the Retreat and what it housed. Cooking, from the use of the stove and the microwave oven to how to build a fire in the wild. Wood was scarce and the search for it had taken Rourke away from the children with the pickup truck to far beyond the base of the mountain. No life—but trees to cut down. Eventually, as the years passed, he had taught Michael to handle the full-sized McCulloch Pro-Mac 610. Rourke's palms had sweated, his stomach churning, letting an eleven-year-old boy handle a chain saw.

Both children he had taught the rudiments of sewing—putting back buttons and mending ripped seams and holes in Levi's. Annie had quickly gotten into the books Rourke had put up for Sarah and by the time she had reached age ten spent much of her leisure time doing needlepoint as she listened to recordings, watched videotapes, and questioned her father.

Marksmanship training for both of them progressed, Annie utilizing the CAR-15 because of the shorter buttstock length, Michael managing one of the M-16s. Target practice in the early years was confined to the .223 because Rourke had such an abundance of ammo for this caliber as well as a large number of M-16s and replacement parts, all of this from the United States Air Force base on the New West Coast, part of the supplies he and Rubenstein and Natalia had brought back with them. Occasional handgun marksmanship was practiced, utilizing miscellaneous .38 Special ammunition fired through Rourke's Metalifed Colt Python.

It was not until Michael reached age twelve that Rourke in earnest began teaching him the use of the .45.

The training gun was the blue Detonics .45 Rourke had taken from the Soviet agent who had worked with Randan Soames near the early site of

U.S. II headquarters. Michael had quickly taken to it. Annie's marksmanship with Rourke's CAR-15 reached such a level that after a time he began joking with her that Annie's real last name should be Oakley rather than Rourke.

The martial arts. Childrens' bodies are supple, strong, flexible—they learned quickly and well, Rourke teaching them the basics of Tae Kwon Doe and letting them progress into other variations. It was not until Michael was thirteen and Annie eleven that Rourke began teaching the children what to do in order to kill with their hands.

He paralleled their instruction, which at times meant holding Michael back, at times pushing Annie forward. But teaching both children simultaneously was the only way for him.

The children studied history. Having lived through its most important epoch, its most pivotal period, they seemed naturally drawn to the discipline. Questions—why had U.S. and Soviet relations fallen to the point where the Night of The War had been the only alternative?

It was then that Rourke showed them something he had begun shortly after the Awakening—it was then that the children had realized why at night he had sat alone in a far corner of the Great Room, music low on the air, a typewriter going. It was a memoir of events leading to the Night of The War, and events afterward. It was not finished and Rourke had confided to his son and daughter that he felt it never would be—there was always more to add.

Shakespeare, Cervantes, Ovid in the original Latin—it was good mental discipline, he had told them.

The sculpture of Michelangelo, the music of Beethoven and Liszt, the philosophy of Aquinas, Sartre, Rand. He realized early on that he was merely introducing the children to things they would have to learn without him.

The fertile soil outside the Retreat yielded corn, potatoes, asparagus, tomatoes, peas. The winters were hard and long and cold and the growing seasons short, but in these times, as in all other times they shared, they shared the work together. John Rourke discovered that he not only had children, he had friends.

They would talk long into the evening—literature, philosophy, music, science, the arts.

Medicine. By the time the last year had begun, both Michael and Annie had learned first aid to the point where either would have been qualified to assume the duties of a paramedic. He had placed medical and dental knowledge above all else but self-defense, for without their health, in this hospitable yet forbidding world, they would perish.

Michael, at nearly fourteen, had begun to seriously assault Rourke's limited—but not too limited—supply of .44 Remington Magnum ammunition. The boy had become enamored of one particular pair of guns. John Rourke had never favored single action revolvers. Michael Rourke favored them.

At the range area beyond the entrance to the Retreat, Rourke stood, watching his son.

Michael, only two inches shorter than Rourke now, held the eight-and-three-eighths-inch-barreled Stalker in both hands at full arms length, the webbed sling for the massive Magnum Sales-converted Ruger Super Blackhawk swaying slightly in the breeze as it hung from its barrel and base-of-the-butt-mounted swivels. John Rourke watched as Michael Rourke studied the target—a pine cone one hundred yards distant—through the 2X Leupold scope. Even with the sound-dampening earmuffs John Rourke wore, the sound of the Stalker as it discharged was intense. In the distance, the dot that had been the pine cone seemed to vaporize as Rourke studied it through the Bushnell armored eight-by-thirtys. "You hit it."

"I know."

"Let's see what you can do with the short one."

"All right."

Michael set down the Stalker, taking the shorter barreled gun from the wooden table they had built together of rough hewn pine logs brought up from the valley below. Michael picked up the Predator. It was largely the same gun, a stainless Ruger Super Blackhawk reworked by Magnum Sales, but this without a scope, the barrel only four and five-eighths inches long.

Michael held the revolver in both hands. John Rourke called to him, "When I sleep again— practice firing that smaller one you've got now,

28

practice firing it faster at closer ranges. Teach yourself to reload it on the run as you fire."

"I understand what you mean, but not how to do it," Michael called back, his voice deeper than it had been as a child. But not as deep as it would be, Rourke thought.

"You take your shot down range—like you planned—then I'll empty it and show you what I mean," and Rourke brought the shooter's earmuffs up again, watching as Michael did the same.

Rourke watched through the binoculars again —another pine cone, this fifty yards away. It was a good-sized pine cone, John Rourke reminded himself as Michael's Predator discharged, the pine cone disintegrating.

Rourke looked at his son—proud, no prouder than when the boy had first attacked geometry and taken quickly to it, but just as proud.

Rourke walked toward his son, leaving the earmuffs up.

Michael handed him the Predator.

"Four shots?"

"Never load more than five in a single action, even if it is a Ruger," Michael nodded.

Rourke smiled. Twenty-five feet away, more or less, was a pine tree that had been struck by lightning—natural lightning. It had happened only six months earlier.

Rourke picked up five rounds of the Federal 240-grain .44 Mags, his right thumb working open the Ruger's loading gate, closing it, opening it, closing. "With an original Colt, I knew a man who kept the loading gate open, reloading just as fast as he fired. You can't do that with one of these. So you improvise."

"Show me," Michael said, his even white teeth showing as his wide mouth opened in a smile.

"I was planning to," Rourke laughed. "That struck tree—that's a man shooting at you. This table is cover. You've gotta nail him as you run toward the table, reloading as fast as you can. Then because there's somebody coming right up your back, you've gotta pass that guy and finish him. So you run from behind cover and empty the next five into him—if it takes that many. This time it will."

"All right."

"Get back over there." Rourke gestured to a rock some distance beyond the table and out of range of any possible missed shot. "And keep your muffs up—shooting's hard enough on your ears in combat, no sense damaging your ears during practice."

"All right."

Rourke took the Predator and the five spare rounds of ammo and strode back perhaps twenty-five feet beyond the table at an angle. He shouted to Michael, "Gimme a yell when you want me to start—and keep in mind I'm not very good with a single action and I don't shoot .44 very often."

"Excuses, excuses—now!"

Michael had caught him flat-footed—but Rourke broke into a run, the Predator in his right fist, the loose ammo in his left, his right thumb jerking back the hammer, the right index finger triggering the shot, the Magnum Sales Custom Ruger bucking in his right hand at the web of flesh between thumb and forefinger, bucking again and again and again as he crossed the distance to the table, the lightning-struck pine shuddering with the impacts, starting to crack near the base, Rourke skidding down behind the table, the loading gate already flicked open. His left thumb worked the full length ejector rod, the loose rounds in the left palm, his left hand's last two fingers holding the Ruger, as the rod reached maximum extension and the empty punched out, his right plucking a loaded round from the palm of his left, inserting it, then repeating the process, the Ruger loaded, the loading gate closed, Rourke up, running, emptying four of the five rounds into the tree trunk target—the tree split, falling.

Rourke stopped running.

Michael was shouting, "That's pretty good, Dad—"

Rourke wheeled, firing the fifth and last round into the remaining stump of the tree, the distance fifteen feet, the stump cracking, a chunk of pine wood perhaps two inches in diameter sailing skyward.

Rourke pulled off his shooter's earmuffs; Michael, approaching, did the same.

Rourke, his voice almost a whisper, said, "I like a .45 better, or a double action. But if you're wedded to these, maybe that's more important. They're good guns."

31

Annie—nearly twelve, shouted from the entrance to the Retreat. "I cracked open the last jar of peanut butter—anybody want a cornbread and peanut butter sandwich?"

Rourke looked at Michael—Michael looked at him.

Annie was turning into a good cook for a girl of her years.

"Come on—peanut butter sandwiches with fresh strawberries and tomatoes and a green pea and asparagus salad. Come on!"

A fine cook, if somewhat bizarre.

Chapter Six

Rourke sipped at a glass of the corn whiskey. The first batch had been too strong, but this was palatable enough. He still had a more than ample supply of civilized Seagram's Seven but almost three years ago had started the still. Michael was planning to produce beer eventually. Rourke had never worshipped beer that terribly much, but if he were nearly fourteen, he supposed that he might—in anticipation.

They sat in the kitchen, Annie talking. "I wish we could find some surviving dairy animals—anything. Even a goat. I've got some great recipes for cheese, for yogurt, and you've got the starters I need. Remember that yogurt I tried with the dehydrated milk?"

"It was good, sweetheart," Rourke told his daughter. She reminded him of her mother, except for the hair color. She had not cut her hair either, not since the Awakening. He mentally corrected himself—occasionally she trimmed "split ends," as she called them. He imagined she had picked up the term from a book or from a videotape. But her hair, when it was unbound as it was now, reached past her waist, still the same dark honey blond color it had always been.

She was becoming a woman—but he would miss the little girl she so rarely was nowadays. He had told her what to expect—when she actually became a woman. For there would be no woman there, no adult.

He had explained to both children what they would feel in their bodies, and explained to both of them the obvious limitations their environment would impose.

But he had planned for that as well. . . .

They sat in the great room, Rourke on the couch, Michael on the reclining chair, but the chair not reclined, the back up straight. Annie sat cross-legged, Indian fashion, on the floor. Behind them—Rourke suddenly noticing it—was the soft hum of the cryogenic chambers. "We six are the future—it's important that all six of us survive to make that future. I haven't really taught you anything, either of you, except the means to improve your skills, to acquire real knowledge.

Sixteen years will pass after tonight before I see either of you again, yet daily each of you will see me, see your mother—she is unchanging. See Paul and Natalia. I'm not leaving you—either of you— an easy task. Not at all. If something comes up for which I wasn't able to prepare you, you'll have to solve it. If it cannot be solved, then awaken me from the sleep and hope that I can solve it. If either of you is so seriously injured that the medical techniques I've taught you and the reference material available cannot alleviate the situation, then awaken me from the sleep. If there is a problem with the Retreat systems which you cannot solve, then awaken me. At even the slightest intimation that the cryogenic systems are failing or the power is failing, awaken the four of us instantly. Instantly."

He looked at Annie. "I want you to pursue your interest in things creative—creativity is vital to survival, mentally as well as physically. Don't redecorate the Retreat—I kind of like it the way it is. But exercise your mind, practice the fighting techniques I've taught you—but don't break your brother in half."

"Dad," Michael laughed.

Annie only smiled.

"Move up from those .38s out of my Python— start into .357 Magnums. Don't get hooked on single action revolvers like your brother."

"I like that Detonics Scoremaster you let me try once—it's pretty and it's accurate."

"Fine—but wait a few years before you get into

34

it, and the gun is yours."

"All right." She smiled, the corners of her mouth dimpling.

He looked at Michael. "I'm not sounding chauvinistic—at least I hope not. But you're two years older, and you're a man. Fourteen is a rough age to start being a man, but you started when you were younger than that and saved your mother's life with those Brigands, helped your mother and Annie out of that swollen lake when the dam burst. You've got an ego I haven't seen the like of since my own. That can be a positive feature if you can control it. A negative feature if you can't. But you'll be in charge. I think Annie accepts that," and Rourke looked at his daughter. She smiled, laughing a little, but nodded. He looked back to Michael. "If I didn't think you could handle it, I wouldn't say you were in charge. You're the one responsible for yourself, your sister and, while we sleep, for the four of us. And when you work with that smokeless powder you're experimenting with, don't blow yourself up." He looked at his son and laughed.

Michael stood up, stabbing his hands into the side pockets of his Levi's, the cuffs turned up because they were Levi's Rourke had put in the Retreat to wear for himself and Michael was not yet his height. "I won't let Annie down—I won't let you, or Mom, or Paul or Natalia down. I don't know how smooth it's gonna go for the next sixteen years, but it'll be all right."

John Rourke stood, Michael Rourke walking

toward him. John Rourke outstretched his right hand to his son. His son took it. Annie stood up, embracing them both. In a few hours, John Rourke would sleep again.

Chapter Seven

The scoped Stalker slung diagonally across his back, Michael Rourke started down from the rocks, into the valley, the Retreat—his father had told him once that Natalia Tiemerovna referred to it as "Rourke's Mountain"—in the distance. He had begun ranging the mountains surrounding the Retreat when he was twenty and in nearly ten years, he had seen no sign of animal life, but the vegetation—where it grew at all—was thicker and lusher with each spring. He quickened his pace— Annie, who had turned into a superb cook, was fixing meat. It was a special-occasion delicacy usually—for his birthday or her own, but this was not January, the month of both their birthdays. Annie, that morning, had simply said, "I'm tired of being a vegetarian—I'm taking some meat out of one of the freezers. Make sure you're not late for dinner."

Michael Rourke hadn't argued.

A rabbit or a squirrel—had he seen one, he would not have shot it, but attempted to follow it.

He would have brought such an animal food from their gardens. But no such animal existed.

No birds flew in the sky. No insect buzzed.

Some type of beetle to attack the vegetables in the gardens would have been welcome, but there were none.

Perhaps in other parts of the world, or at lower altitudes—perhaps.

He had taken one of the three Harley Davidson Low Riders once, taken it far from the Retreat. That had been five years ago. He had ranged for more than a hundred miles in the four cardinal directions. He had found the rusted, gutted remains of an automobile. He had found the ruins of what had once been a city—skeletons of buildings now. Not even a human bone survived.

But the strategic fuel supplies were intact—it had been the announced reason for the trip. He had checked two of the reserves and they still held their precious gasoline.

Annie would range from the Retreat as well at times. He didn't worry that terribly much for his sister. She had begun mastery of the Detonics Scoremaster .45 she had liked so much, begun its mastery when she was fifteen. At twenty-eight—almost—she was a superlative shot. At one hundred yards, without a scope, using just the Bo-Mar iron sight, she could consistently hit objects Michael could barely see with the naked eye.

They had begun reading through the *Britannica* when in their late teens. He had reached the end of volume seventeen of the Macropaedia and found it amusing to read the information concerning tax laws. Taxes were no more.

Michael remembered an expression his father had used once—something regarding the inevitability of death and taxes. Taxes were no longer inevitable. He wondered if death were.

The thought was vaguely disquieting to him that he had known more people who were now dead than still alive. As best he had been able to ascertain in nearly sixteen years of monitoring the airwaves on the Retreat radio, of studying the stars and the daytime sky as well, of searching the ground for the slightest sign, no one else lived on the earth.

He had been tempted once to take one of the Harleys and drive toward Colorado where the Soviet Womb had been. But if anyone had survived there, they would likely be his enemies now as they had been his father's enemies almost five centuries earlier.

At night, when he monitored the radio or studied the stars through the telescope, he would sometimes sit with a glass of the corn-based whiskey—it was quite good now and, at least to him, the taste was as pleasing as the occasional glass of Seagram's Seven; other times he would stare at the cryogenic chambers. Annie would always fall asleep earlier than he, perhaps while they watched a film together on the video recorder. But there were the alone times—and as he watched the cryogenic chambers, he would consider what it would be like when there were no longer just two people walking the earth, but six instead.

As he walked along the mountain road leading to the Retreat now, he wondered again. What was the woman Natalia like?

He remembered from his early childhood seeing his mother and father kiss. From films, he had seen others. One film in particular—the man and the woman lay in bed beside one another. He was not sexually ignorant of the technical aspect of it—he had read, his father in his wisdom having provided things for them both. And before his father had slept, his father had told them both things, answered questions.

But he watched the woman Natalia sometimes, wondering.

And he wondered at his father's remarks about the imperative of all six of them surviving.

Michael Rourke sometimes thought that he thought like his father—and if he did, he realized, then he knew what his father planned and it alternately warmed and frightened him. . . .

"I got the recipe from that cookbook Mom wrote once. What do you think?"

Michael Rourke put down the glass of Seagram's—it was, after all, a special occasion. "I liked it, Annie. What did you call it again?"

"Beef Stroganov. But I didn't have any wine, so I used some of your homemade beer."

"Terrific. The man who marries you—" and Michael Rourke shut up.

He watched his sister's brown eyes, brown like his. She moved her hair—she kept it at waist length—back from her face. "What do you think Dad has planned?" she asked, her voice soft—like Michael remembered his mother's voice being soft.

"You want my honest opinion?"

"Yeah, I want your honest opinion. I'm gonna get dessert. Strawberry shortcake—come on and refill your glass." She stood up, walking back toward the stove and the counter beside it. Michael climbed down from the stool, taking her empty glass as well as his. He passed her, standing at the nearer counter, untwisting the cap on the bottle. "What do you think? You want some more 500-year-old whiskey?"

"Talk about aging! Am I gonna need some more whiskey?"

"Might not be a bad idea."

"All right." She paused. "I'll have some more whiskey. You want a lot of strawberries?"

"Yeah."

He poured the second glass, closed the bottle and turned to watch her as she fixed the strawberry shortcake, ladling freshly cut strawberries which they had grown themselves onto the chunks of cornbread. She was dressed as she usually dressed. Rarely did she wear pants, although she was so talented that she could easily have made more than the few pairs she had fabricated. His father—their father—had provided before the Night of The War bolts of material and thread and a sewing machine and all the necessary accessories. Annie had taken

40

to using the machine like a pianist would take to a concert-tuned piano. He had read about concerts, pianists and the like, watched the videotape of a concert several times. And he listened to music incessantly, as did Annie. But she wore one of her typical midcalf-length full skirts, navy blue in color. And a blouse which seemed to hold up on her shoulders by friction—he had read a novel where such a garment had been described as a "peasant blouse." This was her usual attire. He watched her as she carried the dessert back to the main counter.

He followed her, crossing to the far side of the counter and straddling the stool. He scratched his bare left thigh where it itched beneath the ragged edge of the cut-off Levi's. There were still more pairs of these in the storeroom than he could wear through in a lifetime, but these old ones were comfortable for sitting around the Retreat at night.

"So—what do you think he has planned for us?"

"*Salud,*" he murmured, raising his glass. He had studied Spanish from books and audio tapes and—again his father had provided—watched the one Spanish language movie in the tape library innumerable times.

"*Salud*, already." And Annie clinked glasses with him. "So, what do you think?"

He wished that he smoked, so he could have lit a cigar or cigarette and delayed saying what he felt. "All right." But he didn't smoke. "He always talked about the six of us being vital for survival."

"All right—so?"

"So—you've probably seen me—I've seen you do it—"

"What do you mean? What are you talking about?"

"I'm talking about being human."

"Michael!"

"I think he planned this all along, from the first time that he learned what was going to happen to end the world. That's why he awakened us, spent only five years with us and then slept. He planned it."

"What do you—"

"When you look at Paul Rubenstein, in his chamber—what do you think of?"

"That he's—"

"That's he's a man? The only man who isn't your blood relative?"

Michael Rourke watched his sister. She looked down at her dessert, playing with it with her spoon, not eating it. "I think about that," she whispered. And she looked up then. "And what about Natalia?"

"I think that she's a woman," he answered, his voice almost a whisper.

Michael Rourke looked behind him, at the four cryogenic chambers which dominated the great room—the two others had been put away into the storage area. He looked at the face of the woman Natalia—he remembered something suddenly. Her blue eyes.

Michael turned away—Annie continued to stare

42

at the cryogenic chambers. And he knew what she stared at. "Did he—did he—"

Michael Rourke didn't answer her, his sister.

Chapter Eight

It lasted only a minuscule amount of time, but as soon as it began, Michael Rourke hit the buttons for play and record—the radio made sound.

Words.

As he listened, he tried to understand them—the words—but the language was alien to him.

He checked the Rolex Submariner his father had given him before taking the sleep. The transmission lasted approximately two and one-half minutes.

Annie was already in bed.

The radio had yielded words only twice in all the time he had monitored it. Once nearly five years earlier. Once now.

He had put the words off as an errant transmission bounced back from some object in space. The transmission had been vastly weaker five years ago.

It was strong this night.

"The Eden Project?" he asked himself. Had they come back, entered Earth's orbit? Was it a message? Was it that he could not understand the language? Or that the transmission was so garbled as to be unintelligible, the fault of atmospheric disturbance, or the fault of his equipment?

He had stripped the radio with Annie's help several times, searching—in vain—for some fault in the receiver itself.

There had been none that he could discern.

It was impulse, but he had learned to obey that sometimes.

He snatched up the Predator as he ran across the great room, toward the storage area. His father's Bushnell eight-by-thirtys—he passed them by. The forty power zoom lens spotting scope he used as a telescope. He grabbed this, stuffing it box and all inside his shirt. Pulling aside what blocked the emergency exit hatch, he worked the combination, opening it, and started up through the tunnel along the rungs his father had put in place five centuries earlier.

He kept moving, through the next hatch, not bothering to put the bar in place, merely closing the hermetically sealed door. He kept moving, upward, the exertion making him sweat, the flashlight in his left hand bouncing its beam across the natural rock chimney in the darkness, a white light.

The upper door—he wrenched the bar free, swinging the door open, the cold wash of night air chilling him as he crawled out onto the top of the mountain. He let the hatch swing closed behind him.

Stars—millions, the night cold and crystal clear and the moon little more than a crescent of light.

The box for the spotting scope—he opened it, not bothering with the supporting bipod.

The forty power scope—he zoomed the lens to half of full magnification, searching the horizon.

A streak of light.

Holding his position, he increased the magnification—the streak of light gained definition, clarity, color. Orange, tinged with yellow and red.

It zigzagged. A meteor, he told himself, would not do that. It vanished toward Earth and in his mind he marked the approximate position. Northwest, beyond the mountains, past which he had never ventured, long past these.

Michael Rourke's hands trembled—had they ceased to be alone?

He watched the night sky, shivering with the cold. There was no more light, no further clue.

His voice unsteady—he told himself because of the cold, thin night air—Michael Rourke whispered, "I'll find you."

Chapter Nine

"If it was the Eden Project, it was a crash maybe. And if it wasn't the Eden Project, then it almost had to be some other type of aircraft. That means people—that other people are alive."

Annie licked her lips—she felt strange hearing Michael's words.

She was used to them being alone except for the four sleeping figures in the blue gas swirling cryogenic chambers. She stood up, slipping off the counter stool, stuffing her bare feet into her slippers, her robe and the nightgown beneath it falling past her ankles, the hems brushing the gap of flesh above the banded tops of the slippers. "What do you want to do about it, Michael?" she asked, her voice low, turning to the stove to pour the boiling hot water into the teapot. She grew her own herbs in the garden and made from them an herbal tea which she had become quite fond of. She could smell it as the water penetrated the holes in the small metal tea strainer, and she placed the lid of the china pot in position, twisting it slightly to lock. She would let the tea steep.

"That's what I wanted to talk to you about," she heard Michael saying. She turned around to face him, holding the teapot with a potholder, setting it on the counter beside their waiting cups— Michael tolerated the tea because coffee was a scarce commodity.

Annie gathered her robe around her and eased back onto the stool. "You want to go and see, don't you?"

"Yes—I have to." He reminded her of the memories she had of her father—he looked virtually identical to John Rourke and he sounded identical to him. Her father had made instruc-

46

tional videotapes for them regarding minor surgical procedures, gunsmithing techniques, etc. She played them often so she could remember him. She had no specific memory of her mother, though looking at her in the cryogenic chamber where she slept Annie saw their common physical features. But her mother's hair was darker, auburn colored. Her own hair was, as her father had always called it, a dark honey blond. Specific memories she didn't have, but general memories—love, warmth, friendship. To have another woman in whom she could confide—it was a dream and soon, when it would be the appointed time for the Awakening, it would be reality. She had read books, seen videotaped movies, where mother and daughter disagreed, where enmity had replaced love, distrust replaced respect. It was something she could not comprehend. And yet her mother would be like her sister. Only four years older physically than she when the Awakening would come.

She poured some of her tea, Michael's cup first. "Where will you go?"

"I marked the point on the mountains and when I came back up top I shot an azmuth on it. I can't really be too precise as to the distance. But the direction, I've got that."

"Will you take one of the motorcycles?"

"I can use Dad's maps of the strategic fuel reserves—I'll be all right."

"You can take some of the dehydrated food. I'll prepare it for you. When are you thinking of—"

"Today—in a few hours. If there was a crash and

there's someone out there, well—maybe I can—"

"I know—you sound like our father. You look like him. Sometimes I think you think like him."

He smiled.

"But you don't smoke cigars. I can help you get your gear ready—what will you need?"

"I've got my guns—and I'll take an M-16—"

"Take one of the Gerber fighting knives."

"I was planning to."

"I'll pack some socks and underwear and things for you."

"All right." Michael nodded. "Will you be all right?"

"Alone? But I'm not alone." Annie smiled. "And you've been gone before."

"This'll be for a longer time."

"Give me a time limit—so I know when to start worrying."

Michael Rourke laughed. "All right, if I'm not back in fourteen days, then start worrying."

"If you're not back in fourteen days," and she sipped at her tea—it was very hot, "I'll do more than worry," she promised. The Awakening was to be on Christmas Day and that was seventeen days.

She stood outside the Retreat, the motorcycle—one of the big Harley-Davidson Low Riders, blue—between them. It was cold and she hunched her shoulders under the quilted midcalf-length coat she had made for herself two years earlier, the wind blowing up the road leading away from the Retreat, whipping under her nearly ankle-length skirt, making her bare legs cold where her stockings stopped just below the knee. A shawl—she had crocheted it herself—was wrapped around her head and neck, her hands stuffed in the pockets of her coat.

She watched Michael as he finished securing the last of his gear aboard the bike. She had helped him check it, had prepared a spare parts kit for him just in case.

"Well." Michael smiled. "I guess this is it."

She looked at her brother a moment. He wore one of her father's spare leather jackets. Slung across his back was the Magnum Sales Stalker, scope covers in place. In a crossdraw holster by his left hip bone was the smaller, scopeless, .44 Magnum Predator. She had helped him to secure the M-16 to the bike. On his right hip was the Gerber MkII fighting knife. She had given him another knife from her father's stock—an A.G. Russell Sting IA, but not black chromed like the one that helped to form her father's battery of personal weapons. This was natural stainless steel finish. "I wish you'd take a double action revolver or a semi-automatic pistol."

"I'm happy with these. I know how to use them—even Dad told me I was a good shot with them."

"But Daddy never liked you just carrying single actions—too slow to reload."

"I'll be all right, Annie—now don't worry." He smiled.

She walked around behind the back of the bike, inspecting it once more with her eyes. She put her arms around his neck, felt his arms encircle her body, pulling her close. She wondered what the embrace of a lover would be like. At nearly twenty-eight, she had never known that. She felt Michael's lips brush her cheek. She took his face in her hands, her hands cold in the wind, and kissed him full on the lips, fast. "I love you, Michael—you're the only brother I've got. Be careful."

Michael Rourke laughed. "That the only reason you love me—because I'm the only brother you've got?"

She laughed, burying her head against his chest—the shawl worked down from her head as he stepped away to mount the bike, the wind caught her hair. She raised her arms to capture her hair with her hands, holding it back with her left hand. Michael mounted the Harley and gunned the engine to life.

He looked at her once, smiling. "Be seein' ya, Annie," and then he turned away.

She stood there, the bike starting down the road away from the Retreat, watching him. He looked back once and she waved at him. She kept watching, wrapping the shawl around her head again, stabbing her hands into her pockets, shivering in the wind, but watching him until she could no longer see even a speck of movement that might still be him.

Alone, Annie Rourke turned around and started back into the Retreat, opening the interior door after closing the exterior door, killing the red light and then closing the Retreat door behind her.

In the winter, there was little to do. No garden. She neatly folded her shawl and set it on the edge of the kitchen counter to be put away later. She took off her coat, setting it across the top of one of the stools—the one Michael usually used.

Standing in the cold had made her want to go to the bathroom, and she started across the Great Room. But she stopped, staring at one of the cryogenic chambers. Not her father, or her mother, or the Russian woman Natalia—Natalia was very beautiful. As she—Annie—stabbed her hands into the pockets of her skirt, she stared at another face. Paul Rubenstein. He was not handsome, but she liked the set of his face. She remembered him almost not at all, except that they had all played cards together and Paul Rubenstein had told her she was a very pretty girl and she had giggled.

She smiled thinking of it.

Later she would check the small paper-making operation. Later she would fix a little dinner for herself. Later—later she would go to the bath-room. She stood watching Paul Rubenstein instead.

She was her father's daughter, she had always known, and before Michael had even begun to realize it, she had realized it.

John Rourke had played God.

John Rourke had let her age to nearly the age of Paul Rubenstein. He had picked Paul as her mate, or husband, but who would marry them? Her father? Was being master of the Retreat like being master of a ship? Or perhaps if the Eden Project did return, the commander of the Shuttle Fleet could perform some sort of ceremony.

She had accepted her father's decision, not because it was his decision, but because for some reason she could not understand, she had found herself staring at Paul Rubenstein a great deal, fantasizing what his voice would sound like, wondering if the cryogenic sleep would somehow alleviate the eyesight problem which caused him to wear the wire-rimmed glasses which were with his things in the storeroom. She had washed the glasses once, buffed the lenses. She had wanted to do it.

She looked away from Paul Rubenstein, smiling, laughing a little as she whispered, "My intended." Annie looked at the face of Natalia Tiemerovna. She—Natalia—was her brother's "intended," and Annie knew that. She had considered that a great deal. Michael had talked about their father and "the Russian woman" many times. Annie had decided that her father had been in love with two women—their mother and "the Russian woman."

But something inside of her, and something too in the face of the sleeping "Russian woman" made her feel inside of her that playing at being God wouldn't prove quite as easy as her father might have thought.

She no longer had to urinate. Instead, she started back toward the kitchen—she wondered if Paul Rubenstein would like her cooking. She stopped beside the counter, unbuckling the web belt with

52

the military flap holster from around her waist, the Detonics Scoremaster always carried there when she left the Retreat whatever the reason. She set the gunbelt down beside her shawl, picked up her apron and began tying it about her waist. She could fix something exotic—Michael liked only bland things. A spinach soufflé—she could start with that.

Chapter Ten

He had traveled for five days and in two more would turn back, he had promised himself. He would not abandon the search, but rather return to be with Annie for the Awakening. Then perhaps he and his father both could search, Paul Rubenstein staying behind with the women to protect the Retreat. He had often fantasized what it would be like to rove the new earth with his father, to search out its secrets.

There was his mother to consider, and the Russian woman as well—but he knew his father well. There was something inside his father—and it burned inside him as well.

There was a world to tame, to explore.

Michael Rourke dismounted the Harley Low Rider, letting down the stand, the bike freshly filled some twenty miles back at one of the strategic fuel sites from his father's map. From the cold temperatures and the spectacular height of the mountains and the distance he had traveled, he judged himself somewhere in Tennessee between what had been Chattanooga and what had been Nashville.

There was a high rise of rocky ground with some scrub brush clinging to it for a distance, the rise too steep to navigate with the Harley but not too steep by foot.

He took the key for the Harley, perfunctorily taking the M-16, slinging it across his back, letting the Stalker swing on its sling across his chest as he started up the rocky face. He climbed for a dual purpose—for sign of what he had seen fall from the sky to the northwest and to see if any of the terrain stirred memories in him, memories of the times he and his mother and his sister had moved about these mountains following the Night of The War, searching for his father.

The rocks were a steeper climb than he had anticipated, but he worked cautiously and slowly —a broken ankle or broken leg could have spelled his doom here and he was aware of the hazards of traveling alone in the wilderness.

Michael Rourke kept climbing.

When he reached the top, he sagged over the edge, catching his breath. He wondered what it would be like to function in a full atmosphere again where the air was not so thin and cold in his lungs.

He edged completely over the lip of rock,

standing up. Had it been summer, he would have worn a hat to guard against the stronger sunlight. He ran his hands through his hair instead, reminding himself he would need Annie to give him a haircut when he returned to the Retreat. The wind caught at his hair again and he pushed a thick strand of it—dark brown like his father's, he thought—back from his eyes.

Michael Rourke looked behind him—nothing but landscape, however more beautiful it seemed almost day by day to become. He walked across the flat expanse of rock, taking the Bushnell eight-by-thirtys from their case at his left side—they were his father's.

Before him, as he stopped at the edge of the rock, he thought he might well be able to see as far as the next state.

He focused the rubber-armored binoculars, scanning toward the horizon. Trees were growing in more abundance than he had seen near the Retreat—perhaps being farther north had something to do with it, he surmised—the rays of sunlight less direct, the sunlight level more benign. Michael had placed the binocular strap around his neck, and now he let it fall to his chest.

He took the G.I. Lensatic compass from his leather jacket's left outside patch pocket, opened the case and raised the lens, sighting due northwest. He had no way of knowing if the poles might perhaps have shifted somehow during the cataclysm, the holocaust. But even if they had, he used the compass only for land navigation and it would be consistent for that, if off slightly from true north. The North Star—it seemed where it should be to him when he would scan the nighttime skies.

He picked a mountain top that was due northwest of him, closing the compass, pocketing it.

Michael Rourke raised the binoculars, aiming the twin tubes toward the northwest.

A chill passed along his spine, consuming him with cold. There had been no lightning storms. But there was a thin plume of grey-black smoke rising.

Fire.

"People." He said the word very softly.

Chapter Eleven

He had followed his compass—and by the odometer on the Harley, he had traveled twenty-four miles. For the last two miles, when the rolling of the terrain had permitted, he had seen the plume of smoke, its detail rich, the colors in it varied. He had driven the Harley ever closer to it, his hands sweating inside his gloves.

He had stopped the Harley, taking it off the gravel and dirt track he had followed for the last mile, pulling it into the trees, camouflaging it with pine boughs, taking his pack onto his back, moving ahead on foot. In the clear air, sound traveled long distances. If there were people, he had no desire for a machine from the twentieth century to frighten them. They might well be very simple.

Michael Rourke checked his map, having updated it as best he could as he had traveled, marking on it in faint pencil the coordinates where he had left the bike. He walked on, the Harley's key in his jeans pocket, a duplicate key at the Retreat, the pace he set one that was practiced from walking the mountains near the Retreat, one he could maintain in the thinner air.

His right fist was closed on the Pachmayr-gripped butt of the Stalker. . . .

Michael Rourke walked into the wooded area which for the last mile had been ahead of him, threading his way through the trees, weaving back and forth, moving as soundlessly as possible.

He could smell the smoke now.

And he smelled something else. He didn't know what it was, but it reminded him of the last time his sister had cooked meat. But the smell was not pleasant and warming to him, but somehow vile.

He was afraid.

He kept going.

Michael's fist tightened on the butt of the Stalker, tighter than it had been, the Stalker unslung from his side, held slightly ahead of him but not too far—his father had taught him that a gun extended too far ahead of you was an invitation for someone to try to strike it from your hand. Someone. That there might be someone, besides himself, his sister, their parents, Paul Rubenstein and Natalia Tiemerovna—his stomach churned, his palms sweated and a chill again traveled the length of his spine.

Michael Rourke parted the low pine boughs, their heaviness at this altitude both startling to him and wonderful. He moved in a crouch, the Stalker in his right fist.

The smell.

He stood stock still as he reached the edge of the trees and could see clearly the open area beyond, the clearing. The fire still smoked, in the center of the clearing, blackened and smoldering. The smell was stronger as he moved into the clearing, his eyes riveted to what he saw beside the fire—it was a human femur. White, the flesh gone, the two ends of the bone jaggedly broken.

Michael approached the bone, seeing more bones littering the ground near the fire. He dropped into a crouch—with the spearpoint tip of the big Gerber he carried, he rolled the bone over. The marrow from inside it had been scraped out.

He wiped the knife clean across the clump of grass nearest him, sheathing it.

In the grass, partially charred, lay a fork-sized chunk of meat.

Michael took one of the sticks from the fire—it had evidently been used as a cooking spit, the edges notched. There were two forked sticks on each side of the fire. One end of the stick was sharpened to a point, as if it had been used to

58

thrust through something.

With this sharp pointed end, Michael speared the tiny piece of meat.

He raised it to his nose. The smell was sweet, sickeningly. It smelled like undercooked pork— what little pork had been in the freezer, he and Annie had long ago decided would be cooked and eaten. Rubenstein was, after all, Jewish, as was Natalia partially. Annie had had him helping her while she had cooked the pork, helping her with preserving vegetables grown in the garden. He remembered the smell.

But it was not pork. The bone, like the other bones littered near the fire—it was unmistakably human.

And so was the partially eaten, burned flesh.

He fought the feeling of nausea, standing up, turning away from the fire, trying to breathe through his mouth so he wouldn't experience the smell.

Human beings.

Swallowing hard, his stomach churning, he moved about the clearing. Human feces at the edge of the clearing—the smell still strong. He could have touched them to determine more precisely the age. But warm or not, he would not touch them. A bush, wet, the smell on the leaves that of urine.

He scanned each of the bones as he moved about the place—the encampment.

Michael stopped beside a clump of thorny blackberry bushes. It was what he had searched for.

There were no insects since the Night of The

War, or at least none he had detected. So nothing crawled over it.

He could have picked it up, if he could have reached through the thorny blackberry bush to take it.

But there was no need to take it.

The skin was gone from the top of the thing, as if scalped. Only the facial skin from halfway down the forehead to below the chin remained, the ears gone as well. The eyes were missing. Eaten, he surmised.

The face had been that of a girl younger by some years than his sister.

Now, Michael turned away and threw up, dropping to his knees, lurching forward with his heaving abdomen.

There were people—but they were not people like himself.

They were cannibals.

He had cried as a little boy, but never as a man. Until now.

Chapter Twelve

It was true that the cryogenic process served to regenerate the body.

But not completely. Only one kidney functioned. He no longer had a spleen. A section of his left lung had been cut away. There was a bypass around an irretrievably damaged portion of the large intestine.

But aside from urinating a bit more frequently, and in the thin air tiring a bit more quickly than he would have, he suffered no sustaining ill effects.

He stood, leaning against the fir tree, watching the snow-capped mountain peaks in the distance.

Greater distances away, beyond these mountains and the next and beyond what had been and was still an ocean, lay his desire.

He was confident that destiny had not cheated him.

He had chosen the higher elevations where the air was thinnest for this period of four years since his awakening, chosen it so that he could adapt to thinner air and his decreased lung capacity, so that at normal elevations he would be at full physical strength.

His right hand in his right pocket, he felt at the hardness of his genitalia. He had thought of the woman.

It was time for that.

He turned and walked back from the precipice, along the rugged ground beneath the snow-laden fir trees, toward the mouth of the cave where he and the others had set their encampment three years earlier. He stroked his beard.

He passed through the mouth of the cave and beyond. It was warmer from the solar-battery-generated electric heating coils and he opened his coat, not feeling any shortness of breath as he sometimes did when coming into warmth.

His people were about their business and he was all but alone at the encampment. All but alone. He opened the wooden door of his hut, stepping inside, throwing down his coat, stripping away the shoulder holster and letting it hang from the straight back of the rough-hewn chair beside the table he used as his desk. He allowed the semi-automatic pistol to stay in its holster.

He wouldn't need it, though he practiced with it three times a week at least.

He practiced drawing it quickly from the leather and hitting the torso of a silhouette-shaped target.

He walked from the small room of the hut into the larger room, the only other room. To the left, the shower and toilet behind a curtained doorway built off the room. To the right, the cabinet where he stored the bulk of his possessions.

Ahead of him, the bed.

The girl waited there.

"Do you know what I intend to do?"

She had frightened eyes. She was one of the ones who had survived by some means or another and become more animal than human. But she, the animal, was frightened of him, the man.

She had no language other than grunts and he did not know how to converse with her.

But he spoke with her anyway. "I discovered in myself something very interesting—but this was centuries ago. I was a master of the earth then. A foul-breathed little beast like you would not have interested me then. But you are here."

He picked up the two-foot steel-cored section of rubber hose, etching lines in his imagination with it across the white flesh of her abdomen, then very quickly, raked it hard across her breasts and she screamed.

A scream of pain was somehow a universal language.

He began to undress fully—and then he would beat her well.

Chapter Thirteen

For three days and nights, he had followed them—scraps of burned human flesh, a bone, an occasional footprint—like something wrapped in rags. He had followed the only humans he had found on the face of the earth.

The cannibals.

He had followed them on foot, leaving the Harley at the end of the second day, lest the motorcycle alert them to his presence, lest it deny him the chance of finding humankind, for somewhere inside him, he had told himself that there were at least two species moving on this part of the Earth, the cannibals and their victims. He knew little of cannibal societies on the whole from Earth history, but logic and reason told him that any society, no matter how primitive, no matter how bizarre, no matter how brutal, would require certain rules. And that killing and eating fellow members of the tribe would be taboo—maybe.

The human skull—the female—had seemed normal enough. But then, he had told himself, so too might the cannibals.

The trek after the cannibals was leading him through the mountains, through the very area he had chosen to search for the landing spot or crash site—for the origin of the mysterious light in the night sky, perhaps the origin of the indecipherable radio broadcast.

He had been maintaining a distance of perhaps two miles from the cannibals, never seeing them in more than a fleeting glimpse—a vaguely human shape passing into tree cover. They were nomadic, hunters, without a permanent village, he surmised.

Either that or a long-range hunting party. If it were the latter, then following them would lead to their stronghold or base.

Cautiously, lest he be discovered, he had tracked them, resting when he judged they rested, moving when he judged they moved. They were diurnal in their travel.

As the third day drew into the third night, the scraps of human leavings had all but ceased and no more were there the occasional piles of human feces near the track. They would hunger again.

This night he would close the gap, come up to just outside their camp.

He would see. . . .

Michael Rourke checked the face of the Rolex against the stars. It was nearly midnight. He theorized that his quarry would be asleep now.

He shucked his pack so that he could move quickly, camouflaging it in nearby brush. He debated over the M-16. He had no intention of making battle. He camouflaged this as well, almost hearing his father's voice telling him not to.

But his confidence was in himself and in the two handguns with which he had so often practiced over the years.

He marked this spot's map coordinates, then moved ahead in silence in the darkness.

Silence. He walked quickly, quietly over the rocky terrain, listening each time he stopped, listening for a human voice.

He heard none.

Clouds were moving into the sky on a stiff cold wind and he smelled snow in the air. He kept moving.

Ahead of him, a shadow hung, deeper than the darkness around it.

The Stalker in his right fist, he moved ahead, quietly, listening, toward the shadow.

Michael Rourke stopped in the wooded defile beneath the shadow, the shadow now with form, substance, his left hand reaching up, touching at the harness webbing. He had seen these things in books, seen them in videotapes.

What hung above him snarled in the trees was a parachute, the clouds overhead parting in a sudden and chilling gust of wind, the whiteness of silk or nylon—he wasn't sure which—catching the light from the stars or the moon.

A parachute.

It had been an aircraft he had seen in the sky.

He lit the Zippo lighter he carried to examine the harness webbing. It had been cut cleanly. A knife.

It was from what he had seen fall from the night sky.

The aircraft should be nearby. And so should the pilot. He moved about beneath the parachute, on his hands and knees in the grass and dirt, feeling the dark ground, using the flickering blue-yellow flame of the Zippo sparingly lest he burn down the wick.

A folding knife—nothing unique about it. In the light of the Zippo he read the legend "Rostfrei" and "Solingen" on the blade, but there was no trade name. But the knife—it could not be new—was in perfect condition. He closed the single lockblade and pocketed the folding knife, continuing his search.

He found nothing else beneath where the parachute hung.

He sat on the ground in the cold and the darkness, constructing in his mind what might have happened. If the thing falling from the sky were some sort of conventional aircraft, what he had heard on the radio and what he had heard five years earlier had perhaps been a prerecorded distress signal, perhaps played at higher speed and broadcast toward some base which would have the equipment to ungarble it.

The empty parachute harness, the open folding knife. The pilot had bailed out after sending the message, the parachute snarling in the trees. The pilot had cut himself free. He looked up—the fall would have been perhaps six feet to the ground, but perhaps the pilot had already been injured. It would be the reason for leaving the knife—either that or the approach of the cannibals. But he could not envision even unconsciousness prolonging for more than a week and the pilot simply hanging suspended. He would have left the scene. But if he left the knife, it meant he was injured.

Michael stood beneath the parachute surveying the night around him. The pilot crashed his aircraft, bailing out after sending his distress signal. The pilot's chute became hung up. The pilot was injured in one manner or another and crawled off into the denser trees. Michael moved to his right—down the defile, easier for an injured person to navigate. He followed the gentlest slope, toward the denser growth of trees.

His foot stubbed against something in the dark.

He crouched, shielding the Zippo's flame from the stiffening chill wind. A plastic container, the plastic opaque, heavy, evidently designed for re-use. He smelled the container. A food smell he could not identify.

In the denser tree cover, he could trust to using a flashlight. It was one of the angleheads his father and Paul Rubenstein had taken from the geological supply store in New Mexico—his father had told them the story of the 747's crash more than once, of the origins of his partnership with Paul Rubenstein.

In the beam of the flashlight, Michael scanned the ground, the Stalker slung across his back.

The earth disturbed—he found a sharp stick and dug with it. Human feces. The pilot? The cannibals did not cover their leavings. He recovered the tiny mound.

Another plastic container. In the brush there was the sign of a freshly sawn sapling. But the pine tar had solidified—he judged it as several days old.

He moved deeper into the brush, stopping—his right leg, the shin barked against something hard.

Michael shone the flashlight down. Another sapling, but the entire shaft of the tree. He shone the light beyond it—a lean-to built into the natural brush. Around the lean-to and inside, three more of the plastic containers. A canteen— plastic, late G.I., one quart issue. The kind his father frequently had used when they would be away from the Retreat all day long.

The canteen was empty.

He searched in detail near the lean-to—more of the neatly covered mounds of human leavings.

But where was the downed aviator?

He heard then, over the keening of the night wind, a scream. The first human sound he had heard since Annie's voice when he'd left the Retreat, the first human sound beside his own musings.

He started toward the scream, up the defile, taking a right angle when he reached the tree where the parachute still hung, running now, the Stalker in both hands as he pushed through the trees. The cannibals—perhaps they had the pilot. Snow—he felt it touch his right cheek.

Another scream.

Michael Rourke threw himself into the run. If a civilized man were ahead of him, he had to know from where the man had come. His heart beat—not from the thinness of the air or its coldness, but from something deep inside him.

Chapter Fourteen

Annie Rourke sat up in bed—she was cold.

It was a curious effect of the cryogenic sleep—she and Michael had discussed it. But dreaming, which was so continual, so vivid during "the sleep," seemed somehow to be all but impossible once "the sleep" had been endured. She had consciously dreamed twice since the awakening of herself and Michael. Once on the night her father had returned to the sleep. And this was the second time.

She was aware of the fact that dreaming was frequently subconscious, that one didn't remember the dream or remember having had it. But this was a dream of which she was aware.

Perhaps it was the closeness with Michael, of knowing no other human being for sixteen years—but she could feel inside her that the dream was somehow more than a dream.

She pushed back the covers, standing up, her nightgown falling down around her ankles, not bothering with a robe until she found her slippers in the dark. She found them, then felt in the darkness at the bottom of the bed, finding the robe, pulling it on, belting it around her waist.

She shivered still. She turned on the light beside the bed, its yellow glow bathing the room that her father had built for her in diffused light. She went to the closet—from a hanger she took the heavy knitted double triangle of shawl, throwing it around her shoulders, huddling in it.

She turned off the light, sitting on the edge of the bed in the total darkness, still cold.

Michael. She could not remember the dream. But Michael had been in great danger. She shivered.

She stood up, walking in total confidence in total darkness across her room. Just outside the door was one of the switches for the lights which illuminated the Great Room.

She hit the switch.

She walked down the three steps from her room toward the four operating cryogenic chambers.

It was nearly Christmas anyway.

First her father, then her mother, then Natalia, then—she studied the face as she activated the switch. "I'll finally know you." Paul Rubenstein.

It would be several minutes before they began to awaken—running, she took the three steps to her room. She wanted to change into something pretty. She threw the shawl down onto the bed and began to rummage through her closet.

Chapter Fifteen

He had run into it, not slowing, the snow covering the ground in spots now, the cold wind blowing the snow like tiny icy needles against his skin, the fire at the center of the clearing flickering, the flames licking skyward into the cold darkness, the screaming again. A woman—a human woman. She screamed once more and was silent, the instrument in the hands of the cannibal dripping crimson with blood in the firelight as her executioner turned.

The woman's guts spilled to the ground.

Michael Rourke raised the Stalker in both fists, shouting, "Freeze!"

The cannibal raced toward him, shouting something barely intelligible—but it sounded like "Meat!"

Michael Rourke thumbed back the hammer. He had taken human life, but it had been centuries ago. "So help me—freeze!"

The cannibal kept coming. There were others—at least two dozen. In the flickering of the bonfire—the smell of human flesh in the smoke as the wind died for an instant—there were bodies tied to trees. An arm was missing from one of them, and a man—was it a man really—at the fireside held the thing—the arm—to his teeth. There was a human form dead on the ground. But it wasn't dead. It was moving and there was a scream—the skin was being peeled away from the flesh with a wedge of rock.

Michael Rourke pulled the trigger, the 240-grain lead hollow point making a tongue of orange flame in the gray-black night as the Stalker rocked in his fists. The center of the cannibal's face collapsed, blood and brain matter spraying in a cloud on the air, the fire hissing and steaming with it.

A scream, almost inhuman, and then the shrieked word, "Help!" Michael Rourke wheeled right, a woman there. She had shouted in English. Naked, tied to a tree, one of the cannibals falling upon her, his teeth catching the glint of firelight, yellow, saliva dripping from his mouth as he started to bite at her right breast and she screamed again. Michael jacked back the Stalker's hammer, firing, the big customized Ruger rocking again in his hands, the cannibal's body jerking away from the woman as if caught in some irresistible wind. Michael felt it on the hairs at the back of his neck—grateful Annie hadn't cut his hair.

He wheeled, backstepping. The Stalker not

raised to his line of sight yet, he jerked the trigger, a cannibal with a stone axe less than six feet from him, the axe making the downswing, Michael feeling the rush of air as the scoped .44 Magnum rocked in his fists. The cannibal's body jackknifed, feet off the ground, the body rolling back in midair, falling. Michael slipped the Stalker's sling over his head and his right arm through it, letting the pistol fall to his side, grabbing the smaller, more manueverable Predator in his right fist, firing as another of the cannibals charged at him.

The woman on the far side of the fire with the missing arm—she was dead.

The man on the ground with his skin being severed from his flesh—beside him was one of the plastic food containers, half spilled from a rucksack. The container was still full. These people wanted only living flesh as food.

He backstepped toward the still-untouched woman—she screamed again and he wheeled, firing, the cannibal from the fireside, swinging the arm of the human female over his head like a club, Michael's slug splitting the cannibal's skull at the center of the forehead.

And then he felt the feeling rising in his stomach. The cannibals—their bodies were clothed in human skins. The man he had just shot, his upper body and his loins were wrapped in it, the upper portion of a human face, long red hair hanging from it, almost obscene but more than obscene, swaying over his crotch as the wind caught at it. The human skull. The dead woman—

her eyebrows had been an almost unnatural red.

"Fuck you all!" Michael shouted the words, his throat hoarse with them—he pulled the Predator's trigger again, then again, then again. One shot remained, the action cocked under his thumb as the just-shot bodies rocked on the ground. By the fireside, others of the cannibals had fallen on two of the bodies, ripping arms and legs from the torsos, running with them into the shadow.

Rourke heard the woman scream from behind him. "No!"

He spun ninety degrees right. His father had been right, a single action—he pulled the trigger from hip level, the cannibal's hands clasping at his chest as the body rocked back and away—was too slow to reload.

Michael stabbed the revolver—empty—into the crossdraw holster, finding the butt of the big Gerber knife. He wheeled toward the woman, hacking the blade outward—the ropes binding her hands to the notch of the tree above her, the rope made of twisted vines, blood oozing from her right wrist as she fell to the ground.

He reached for her, drawing back as he saw the shadow from the firelight lunging forward. He buried the big fighting knife into the neck of one of the cannibals and drew it back.

He hacked at the vine rope twisted around the woman's ankles. Woman? She was only a girl.

The girl raised her head—her eyes looked blue in the firelight. She was the first totally naked woman he had seen in his life.

"Who are—"

"Michael. Let's get the hell out of here."

"The archangel Michael—the sword—"

Her eyes—they seemed riveted to the knife in his right hand.

Another of the cannibals, Michael dragging the girl up, but only to her knees, his right hand hacking out in a wide backhand arc, blood spurting as the blade snagged at the carotid artery of the lunging cannibal. The body fell back, blood making a fine cloud in the cold wind. Michael dragged the girl to her feet.

"Can you run?"

"I'm naked."

"I noticed—run for it!" And he shoved at her, the girl starting forward, Michael shouting, "Back that way—hurry!"

He looked back once—another of the cannibals. Michael swung the knife toward him. The cannibal stepped back, then ran toward the fire, falling onto one of the bodies.

Michael Rourke turned, running after the naked girl before he lost sight of her in the darkness. Had she come in the plane?

Why had she called him "archangel"?

His heart pounded in his chest harder than it had ever pounded before. But he kept running. Once he reached the Retreat again—if he reached the Retreat again, *when* he reached the Retreat again—he would take a third handgun. One that loaded faster.

Chapter Sixteen

Natalia Anastasia Tiemerovna sat up—so suddenly her head felt light and she closed her eyes.

To her left was Paul Rubenstein. He had not yet sat up. She could tell because the cryogenic chamber's lid was not yet elevated.

To her right was John Rourke. "John," she whispered, her voice sounding, feeling odd to her. The lid of his chamber too was closed, but she could see him stir inside. He was alive. Beyond John Rourke, in the farthest chamber, Sarah sat up, rubbing her eyes.

Natalia closed her eyes—the children. "The children—where—" and she looked at the face that held the eyes that looked at her. The eyes were brown, like John Rourke's eyes. The hair, it was a dark honey blond, very long it seemed, draped over the girl's left shoulder and to her waist and beyond.

The girl. "Who? Annie?"

"Natalia—rest. We can talk. All of us can—"

Natalia looked to her right—she had moved her head too fast. Annie was talking. "I think women wake up faster from cryogenic sleep than men do—just like they do from regular sleep, I guess."

If Annie were an adult, Natalia thought—thinking was hard. She tried to organize her thoughts. John Rourke, there was some little gray in his hair, more than she remembered. She watched as he stirred.

Natalia turned to Annie, trying to move her legs. She could not move them yet. "How old is Michael?"

"He'll be thirty in less than a month," Annie's soft alto answered in almost a whisper.

"Thirty—he's—" Natalia looked at John Rourke—he stirred more, seemed about to open his eyes. "John, why?" Natalia sagged back against the chamber's pillow and closed her eyes. She wanted to weep but no tears would come to her—yet.

Chapter Seventeen

Natalia had spoken almost not at all. Sarah had hugged Annie to her, but had said nothing.

Paul had asked questions. John Rourke had answered them, Annie answering some of the questions. Rourke watched his daughter's eyes as she spoke to Paul Rubenstein. And he watched Paul's eyes—Paul could see without his glasses.

Natalia had been sick. Sarah, too—Paul as well. Rourke, more knowing what to expect, had taken the reactivation of his plumbing in better stride.

Annie had reset his watch and he stared at the luminous black face of the Rolex now—the awakening had come some time after midnight. It was nearly nine a.m. and he was trying some of

Annie's herbal tea, sipping at it slowly.

He sat on the sofa in the great room. Annie sat on the floor, her legs vanished under the nearly ankle-length blue skirt she wore as she knelt near his feet. "You don't believe in dreams, do you? I thought I raised you to be more level-headed than that." Rourke smiled. The herbal tea tasted nauseating, but the coffee shortage to consider, he had decided at the first sip to drink enough tea to develop at least a tolerance for it.

"I've had two dreams since I awoke from the sleep, Daddy. The one dream was about seeing you and Momma again—awake. The other dream was about Michael in danger. And I'm seeing you and Momma awake right now. And Michael's been gone from the Retreat for eight days."

"You said he'd told you he'd be back in fourteen days, Annie."

"I felt it, Daddy—please. Go look for him."

John Rourke sipped at the tea. "I intend to. By midday, my stomach should be stabilized and I should feel stronger. By tomorrow, I should be able to go after him."

"Not without me—and my stomach's killing me." John Rourke knew the voice. He looked at Annie's face instead as she looked up. He watched her hands as she smoothed her skirt with them, as she touched at her hair with them.

"All right, Paul." Rourke nodded, not looking at the younger man—he was five years younger still. "The ladies will be safe here at the Retreat—"

"I'm going, John. You made it so that Michael

would be the right age." Rourke turned around. Flanking Paul Rubenstein were Natalia and Sarah.

"What do you mean?" Rourke said to Natalia.

"You stole my children," Sarah hissed. "You stole them from me forever. Maybe you plan to make me pregnant again—so we can repopulate the world. But you stole these children. You stole Michael and Annie. They're grown up."

"And you think that you solved our problem, don't you?" Natalia said emotionlessly. "You pandered me to your son. How could you, John?"

John Rourke looked at his hands—they were steady. "For all I knew, for all I know, there are six human beings alive on Earth. Maybe the Eden Project will return. Maybe some other people have survived. Maybe Michael is confronting them right now. Maybe. But six people. Six people. Definite. I love both of you," and he looked at Sarah and then at Natalia. "I did what I did out of love, for our survival."

John Rourke stood up. There should be quite a lot of the cigars remaining—he started, his legs still weak, across the great room, toward the kitchen and the freezer where he kept them. Behind him he heard Natalia's voice, "I love you— not someone the age that you were, not someone who looks like you, not your son."

Rourke stopped at the height of the three steps leading to the kitchen. He leaned against the counter. "I did the only thing I could do. Now leave it alone," he almost whispered.

Sarah's voice—he didn't look at her. "Which god are you, John?"

His voice welled up inside him and he shouted without looking at her, "Leave it alone!"

"Which god are you? Which god are you, John Rourke! Should I fall on my knees to you? Should I burn a goddamned sacrifice to you? If you make me pregnant again, should I sacrifice our first born to you—you already made me sacrifice two children!"

"Alone! Leave it alone!"

"No!"

"Momma!"

"Stay out of this, Annie—"

"Mrs. Rourke, Sarah—"

"No. You worship him—it's written all over your face. He's your big macho hero—taught you how to ride a bike, how to shoot a gun. Well, nobody goddamned taught me. He wasn't there with me." Rourke turned around, watching Sarah now as she turned toward Natalia. "And you love him because you're like him—you're both better than human beings, better than anybody at anything. You were made for each other. But he didn't steal your children from you. You don't have the memories of them inside you, of caring for them when the world was going to hell, of smuggling them past Russian guards when they were naked and shivering under blankets, of fighting and killing to keep them alive. I went through all of the hell—and now he took them!"

John Rourke watched his wife's eyes. "You did

this all because you know what's right for everybody, don't you? You'd stay away for days building this Retreat. You'd keep at it and at it making this—this place. Well, what good did it really do? We're alive and to keep the damned human race going you played god and made the children grow up so your son could marry your mistress and your daughter could marry your best friend. How fucking noble!"

She turned away, walking into the bedroom he had built with his hands for them to share.

The door slammed.

He felt something—a presence and he looked away from the closed door. Annie stood behind him, on the lowest step. She wrapped her arms around his waist. "We started to raise tobacco, and in the encyclopedia and in the other books, I learned how to make cigars for you. I've been freezing them for years. You can smoke all you want. Just like the Cuban ones—rolled on the lips of—" She licked her lips, looking over her shoulder at Paul Rubenstein. Paul stood there, his hands in his pockets, Rourke watching as the younger man stared down at his feet. He'd never seen Paul Rubenstein's face so red before.

"I love you, Daddy. I know what Momma meant. I'd hate you if you took away my children, but I'm not Momma. And I love you. Hold me," and she rested her head against his chest as she ascended the steps.

John Rourke held his daughter close against him and closed his eyes. A long time later, he smoked one of the cigars and the taste—different than his other cigars—was somehow better.

Chapter Eighteen

He was still stiff and his muscles sore, but on the trail in pursuit of Michael there would be time to regain his strength from his long sleep.

At least Paul Rubenstein told himself that as he stood in the workroom, fieldstripping the Browning High Power. The magazine out, he drew the slide back and locked the safety in the forwardmost notch. He began working the slide stop out until he could pluck it from the left side of the frame with his fingers. Slowly, he lowered the safety on the worn 9mm, letting the slide move forward and dismounting it from the rails. He removed the recoil spring and guide from the inverted slide, then jiggled out the barrel.

He heard the rustle of clothing beside him. He looked to his left—it was Annie. "I guess your mother was kinda angry," he told her, not looking at her but looking at the pistol again. He took the Break-Free CLP and began to pour some of it—the cap removed—onto a rag to degum the pistol.

"You're the only eligible man in the world. But that's not why I fell in love with you, Paul."

He swallowed hard. "Hey, don't make fun of me."

"What did you look like with your glasses on?"

"I don't know. Maybe my eyes being normal is just temporary. Maybe—"

"Daddy—my father—he had scars from old wounds and they healed."

"My left arm—there isn't any scar from that spear. You'll have to get your father to—"

"He told me. You're a very brave man."

Paul Rubenstein laughed. "Bullshit. I'm just—well, I pick things up quick. Your father—he's the one—"

"You're a brave man. He told me you saved his life more than once."

"No, I never did that. I just—and anyway, God, John saved me—I mean, your father, he—"

"When Daddy told you about your mother and father—what that Colonel Reed told him—I wanted to hold you."

"Annie, you're a little—"

"I'm a woman—and I fell in love with you while you slept. Not because Daddy made things so I would. I just did. Like girls falling in love with movie actors or rock singers—never meeting them. I fell in love with you."

"That's not love, that's—"

"He told me about the girl in New York once—one night. He was up very late and I was ten years old and I sat up with him and he told me all about you."

"The Eden Project—there'll be lots of guys,

guys a lot better—"

"I'll be a spinster then, if you won't have me."

He realized he was moving the cleaning rod in and out of the barrel and he thought she might think he was thinking something he shouldn't think and he set the barrel and the cleaning rod down and he looked at her. "I, ahh—"

"You want to say you don't love me yet—and I understand that."

"Gimme a chance to breathe—"

"I know that—but I wanted you to know before you go off after Michael. I couldn't just not tell you," and she leaned up toward him, Paul feeling her hands touching at his face. She was very pretty—the deepness of the brown of her eyes, the hair was unimaginable, like something from a fantasy about a mermaid or a goddess, he thought. The white blouse—it showed the bareness of her shoulders where the shawl she wore fell away from her.

"You're the daughter of my best friend. He—"

"That has nothing to do with it."

"You're a gentile, I'm—"

"That has nothing to do with it—there aren't any rabbis and there aren't any ministers."

"But—"

"But?"

He licked his lips. "Annie—you—Annie—"

"I fell in love with you. I used to fantasize what your voice was like because I couldn't remember it. It's soft—I like it."

"Annie—"

"When I was seven or so and we played poker that night, you told me I was pretty."

"You're beautiful. You're the most beautiful woman I ever—"

"I'm your woman. I don't expect you to do anything. But when you want to—just—I never talked like this. I'm your woman."

"You're—"

"Almost twenty-eight."

"You're—"

"You're almost five hundred and twenty-eight," and she laughed.

"I'm not that—" and he laughed.

"Daddy told me you were kind of quiet. I think he meant shy."

"Aww, dammit, look—"

"All I wanted was for you to know—that I'll be here when you get back, Paul."

"Annie—look—"

"I looked—for a very long time," and she leaned up suddenly and he realized she was standing on her toes and her lips touched his cheek and she was gone, walking away. He watched how she wrapped the shawl about her shoulders.

He licked his lips. He looked back to the worktable.

Paul Rubenstein closed his eyes. He couldn't remember how to put the parts together. Of the gun.

Chapter Nineteen

They had spent the night hiding in the trees, the woman saying nothing, shivering, wrapped in the Thermos blanket from his back pack and inside the sleeping bag as well, Michael with the M-16 beside him, the two revolvers fully loaded. He had broken his cardinal rule and kept sixth rounds in each of the cylinders but would remove them before moving on.

Daylight had come after the fireless night.

The woman talked in her sleep, but neither was she intelligible to him nor was the language the language from the tapes he had made of the radio broadcast.

Michael had wanted to awaken her.

Had she come with the pilot?

Where was the pilot from?

Who were these people who craved human flesh?

Were there more of them?

He could not ask her because she did not awaken.

She had raced through the trees, Michael grabbing her, dragging her in the right direction, toward the spot where he had secured the pack and the rifle, past the hanging parachute—mute testimony to what, he wondered.

He had covered her body with his coat and his shirt, the snow freezing his bare skin.

They had reached the bracken of pines and the

brush beyond and he had wrapped her in the blanket, found a fresh shirt for himself, taken back his jacket, wrapped her in the sleeping bag.

He had kept her warm while he sat on guard, unsleeping, freezing as the snow piled high around them.

Once there had been sounds. There were no animal forms on the earth that he had seen—except his family, except this woman, except the cannibals, whoever they were. But the sound had been the wind, he had reasoned, because it had returned several times in exactly the same way and there had been no attack.

But he had stayed ready throughout the night.

And then the woman spoke to him. "You are the archangel."

He looked at her, saw the smile etched across her face—one of peace. But her eyes were already closed again and she was asleep.

She no longer moaned and mumbled in her sleep and Michael Rourke watched her for a long time. There was nothing else to do and under the dirt smudges on her face, she seemed pretty to him. It was how one perceived another human being—he had long ago thought that through. And he perceived her as pretty, as terrified. And he perceived her as safe from those people who would have done their foul things to her—for as long as he had breath.

The cold helped him stay awake because it made his body tremble.

Chapter Twenty

"I'm not some archangel—I just have the same name."

"But you are not one of Them, and you are not from the Place. The other one—he was an angel, that is why he fell from the sky. And you came to save him—and you saved me, too. I am sorry. Was he your friend?"

"The pilot?"

"The other angel, his name was Pilate—like Pontius Pilate. I would think an angel would have a name that was less like that weak man's name—Pilate. I am sorry for your friend, Archangel Michael."

Michael Rourke closed his eyes. "This is a fighting knife," and he showed her the Gerber. "It isn't some heavenly sword."

She smiled. Her eyes were still very pretty. "We were taught to call your mighty blade a sword. But I shall call it a fighting knife if you wish that, Archangel Michael."

"I'm not an archangel. I'm not even a regular angel—I'm just a man."

"You are not Them, and you are not from the Place. The angel Pilate came down from the sky and you came to rescue him—you are obviously the archangel Michael. You told me that you were Michael."

"I am Michael," and she smiled as he said it. "But—"

"When must you return to heaven?"

"I, ahh—"

"Please, I know that I'm not worthy of heaven—but don't leave me here. Slay me with your avenging sword, perhaps—anyplace but to be here with Them and alone."

"Them?"

"The ones who consume the flesh. Them. They fight those from the Place."

"I can take you back to the place."

The girl—he didn't yet know her name—fell to her knees and folded her hands and touched her forehead to her hands. "Archangel Michael, do not return me to the Place. I beg this by all that is holy. They will give me back to Them. Do not return me to the Place—do not for they will give me to Them, slay me. I pray."

Michael Rourke looked at her—she prayed to him. She called him an archangel. She was from the Place. She was afraid of Them. But who was she? he thought. "I'll go with you. You'll be safe."

She looked up, settling back on her behind—the blanket was all that was around her. "Archangel Michael is good."

Michael Rourke watched her eyes a moment. "Sure."

Chapter Twenty-One

John Rourke stepped out of the Retreat and into the cold sunlight. There was snow on the air—he could smell it. Sarah had told him one thing and only one . . . "Bring Michael home to me." The bikes were already outside, Annie and Paul talking, apparently, down the road a bit from the Retreat doors.

Beside Rourke stood Natalia Tiemerovna. He didn't look at her as she spoke. "I had to go with you. Sarah and Annie—they need time to know each other. And I couldn't stay here now."

He looked at her. "Are you angry at me, too?"

"You are a good man—your heart is good. But you don't understand the human heart. I'm sure you could perform bypass surgery on the heart if you had to, but you don't understand it. What you did may have been right objectively, but to Sarah it will always be wrong. Do you really want me to become Michael's wife?"

"That's part of why I did what I did, allowed the children to age while we slept."

"You didn't answer my question." He had looked away again, and he felt her hands on his arms now and he turned around to face her—her eyes. "Do you want me to be some other man's wife? Even if the other man is your son? Do you?" He didn't answer her. "I was always certain of one thing since I first met you, I think. That I love you and that you love me. Do you want to think about your son loving me? Do you want to come to hate us both, or to hate yourself?''

"From what Sarah said, I should hate myself already, shouldn't I?''

"Do you want me as someone else's wife? Do you?''

It was very cold in the fresh air after so long. "No.''

"I looked to you like a god,'' she whispered, barely audible as the wind rose from the northwest. "My uncle, he told me that you were not a god, that you would never consider yourself a god.''

Rourke looked away. "All I tried to do—'' he began.

"I think the reason I felt what I felt, what my uncle spoke about—I have never met a human being so perfect.''

He looked at her. "I'm not—''

"But you are—and the perfection is your flaw, John.''

"You sound like you're analyzing a tragedy.''

"Perhaps I am, John. You were always able to subordinate your humanity to your logic. And you did it one time too often. You wanted to love me—physically. But you would never allow yourself to. But because of your humanity, your perfect logic hurt you. In trying to do what you logically deduced was the impartial, the correct thing, you made the most subjective decision any man has ever made.''

Rourke laughed—a short laugh. "I kinda

screwed up, huh?"

"I love you with all of my heart. I'll always love you that way. And I'll do your will if that is what you choose."

"Michael." Rourke smiled. "He's, ahh—"

"Not you. He couldn't be. No matter how like you he is—no matter what he looks like, Annie said he looks just like you. No matter what is in his heart or his mind—he's not you."

He raised his eyes—he'd been studying the toes of his combat boots in detail, the added coats of polish he'd given them before the last sleep had preserved them perfectly. Some of the spare pairs of combat boots in storage—he should look to them, he reminded himself.

"I never planned for falling in love with you," he told her simply. "It changed so—it—"

"Sarah will be so happy when she sees Michael, when she gets to know Annie. She'll—"

He closed his eyes. "No, she won't. He's a man now—I took her little boy. I took her little girl."

"You and Sarah, you can have—"

"I don't think so," Rourke answered, lighting one of his new cigars in the blue-yellow flame of his battered Zippo. "I don't think so."

"But she loves you—"

"If we're going to make any time while there's still daylight—"

"John—"

Rourke looked away from her. He didn't know what to say and there wasn't much point in saying anything at all, he felt. "No point at all," he

92

told the wind.

Chapter Twenty-Two

Rather than going back to where he had hidden the Harley, they had walked, the girl—she was very pretty—telling him the Place was less than a day's journey from the spot where they had spent the night. The snow and the cold made more permanent shelter imperative, Michael Rourke had reasoned—and his curiosity at finding the nature of her people was something he realized to be insatiable. She had had no clothes and from his things and with his help she had fashioned some. His spare pair of Levi's was too hopelessly large for her; but with a cut of rope she had fashioned a belt and the Thermos blanket had become an ankle-length skirt. She wore one of his spare shirts and his sweater against the cold, his sleeping bag like a coat. With part of the butchered Thermos blanket and a little more of the rope, she had fashioned coverings for her feet, and in addition to these wore two pairs of his boot socks.

She seemed physically fit, healthy—the pace she set was a quick one as they moved out of the woods, widely circumventing the clearing where the cannibals had held her and nearly killed her.

He watched her hair as it caught in the wind—it

was a golden blond color, like the yellow of the sun and cascaded in waves to the middle of her back. She turned around suddenly—he guessed she somehow knew he was watching her. She smiled and the pale blue of her eyes struck him. "You're very beautiful," he told her.

She laughed. "The Archangel Michael is very kind, but I am not beautiful." Her face was thin, but not unpleasantly so—it was youth, he decided.

"How old are you?"

"I have nineteen years—that is why it was my time."

"Your time?"

"To be sacrificed to Them."

Michael had no idea what she was talking about. He suddenly realized that he had never asked her name. "What's your name?"

She laughed again. "Only the Families have names."

"You have to have a name. What do they call you?"

"Who?"

"Your friends—the other people?"

"Oh, I am Madison. But then so are many others. The numbers change when one goes."

"What do you mean—goes?"

She stopped walking, putting her tiny, long-fingered hands on her hips. "The Archangel Michael must know what it means when some person goes. You laugh at me."

They were coming into some rocks. They had been walking for two hours by the position of the sun. He glanced at the Rolex on his left wrist—it was two hours and fifteen minutes. "Let's rest for a few minutes before we go on," he decided, starting toward the rocks, talking to her still. "And I told you—I'm not an archangel, my name is Michael, but it's Michael Rourke."

She laughed. "That must be why you do not know what it means when someone goes. In the language of heaven, Rourke must mean Archangel. In the language of the Place, goes is like—well, whatever it would be in the language of heaven."

He found a flat rock and sat on it, the girl dropping to a slightly lower rock beside him, tucking her knees up almost to her chin, gathering the improvised skirt around her legs.

"When someone goes," he persisted. "What happens?"

"You joke with me again, Archangel Michael."

"I'm—" He started to tell her he was not an archangel. Instead, he said, "For convenience sake, just call me Michael."

"Like, ohhh, like you called the other angel Pilate. I feel this is disrespectful for me not to call you Archangel Michael."

"It isn't disrespectful, believe me."

"Michael—Michael," she repeated, smiling. "I like the sound of Michael."

"What do they call you?"

"When I learned that Madison twenty-four goes I became Madison fifteen."

"Madison fifteen?"

"One is born a Madison and assigned an immaturity number, but then at the age of eight one is given a maturity number. I was Madison twenty-nine, then I was Madison nineteen, then I was Madison four. I am now Madison fifteen. But I am probably not Madison fifteen anymore. When someone is sacrificed to Them, the person goes and their number is reassigned."

"Then you're just Madison." Michael Rourke smiled.

She appeared to consider this. "Yes, Michael. I am Madison."

"What are some of the other names at the Place?"

"Among the Families or among the people like myself?"

"Like yourself, for openers."

"There are Hutchins, Greeleys, Cunninghams —many like that. There are many Cunninghams but they work in direct contact with the Families."

"Madison—who are the Families?"

"The Families own the Place."

"What are some of their names?"

"One of the Families is called the Vandivers. Another is called the Cambridges. Another is—"

He cut her off. "And these people have first names. I mean like Michael is a first name."

"Oh, yes, Michael—once I served Elizabeth Vandiver in her suite. I carried in her wedding dress along with several of the other Madisons."

He puzzled over this a moment. "What do the Madisons do?"

She laughed. "What Madisons always do. Make the clothing, clean the clothing, repair the clothing, take the wrinkles from the clothing, fit the clothing. But only two of the Madisons do this—fitting."

"Just for the women or—"

She laughed again. "The Hutchins do this for the men—they fit the clothing. But the Madisons do all the rest."

"You're a servant."

"Of course. I am a Madison."

"All Madisons do this?"

"Yes, Michael—what else would a Madison do?"

"Who does the cooking?"

"The Callaways."

"The Place—who cleans it?"

"We keep things clean among ourselves—but for the Families?"

"Yes—for the Families."

"The Cunninghams—they clean and serve and—"

"What do the Families do—like this Elizabeth Vandiver?"

"Do?" and she laughed.

"Yeah—what do they do?"

"Miss Elizabeth Vandiver paints, and she raises orchids. But, of course, she is Madame Elizabeth Cambridge now. She supervises her household."

"You have two classes—the masters and the servants."

"Yes." She nodded.

"Why?" Michael asked her.

"Why?"

"Yeah, why?"

"It is always this way."

"When someone goes—it's always to Them?"

"No," and her face lost its smile. He noticed her dimples by their absence from the corners of her mouth. Her lips were thin, pale. Her hands trembled and he didn't think it was the cold. "A very little one goes sometimes—it is not known why. And the very old ones. When it is time, each of them goes. And when a new one is born someone always goes. When Madame Elizabeth had her baby, I thought it would be my turn for sacrifice. And it was."

Michael Rourke closed his eyes, opened them, focusing on the toes of his combat boots. "How many people live at the Place?"

"One hundred," she answered.

"About a hundred, huh?"

"Exactly one hundred." It was the first time he had heard her use any word even similar to exactly.

"What do you mean—exactly a hundred?"

"There are never more than a hundred—except for a few hours after a young one is born. Sometimes there are less than a hundred, but then new ones are born."

"Exactly a hundred. Young and old, male and female?"

"Yes—why do you take such interest, Michael?"

Cannibals lay outside the Place. Inside, he

98

realized, there was likely something much worse. Systematic genocide with willing victims.

He reached out his left arm, putting it around the girl's shoulders, drawing her close against him as they sat beside one another on the rocks. "You'll be safe, Madison," Michael Rourke almost whispered. "Safe."

Chapter Twenty-Three

John Rourke ran his bare fingertips across the ground—it was the faintest of tire impressions. He stood to his full height, stiff still from the cryogenic sleep but feeling his strength return. He didn't look back. "Michael's been this way. He must be following a straight northwesterly course."

"He cannot—the mountains," he heard Natalia interject.

"It doesn't matter which way he picks around an obstacle—he'll pick up the same course on the other side. If we lose all track of him, Paul can go one way, you and I the other," he told her, pulling on his gloves against the cold, turning, walking back toward the bikes. Natalia stood beside the jet-black Harley. Paul rode his own bike. The blue Low Rider Rourke had taken from the Brigand camp was the machine Michael rode. "You've gotta remember," Rourke told them, mounting the Harley, putting his dark-lensed aviator-style sunglasses back to cover his eyes. "I taught him land navigation—I taught both of them. But this is his first time any great distance from the Retreat. He'll be smart enough to stick to the basics, even if it means going out of his way a little. Anyway— he'd stick northwesterly because he's trying to pinpoint that crash site or whatever it was."

"The messages on the tapes—or whatever they were. Could you figure out the language?" Paul asked.

Rourke looked at Rubenstein, feeling Natalia mounting the Harley behind him, feeling her arms circle his waist. "Yeah. It was some sort of computer message. I'd need the access code to figure it out."

"The Eden Project?" Natalia's voice asked from behind him.

Rourke twisted in the saddle, looking at her. "No, this is something else. I don't know what— not yet. But if something crashed out there, well, we'll see," and Rourke shoved the CAR-15 back on its sling, gunning the Harley, feeling the machine as it vibrated under him. "Let's go, Paul," he called.

There were still a few hours of daylight. After the cryogenic sleep, he would not feel he needed sleep, but he was tired from the exertion. So long without exercise or proper nutrition.

He let out the Harley—to follow his son.

Chapter Twenty-Four

"I have never eaten flesh—it is forbidden. Them, they eat flesh."

Michael looked at the jerked beef stick in his right hand. "Used to be, I remember it a little—before the Night of The War—"

"Between the angels?"

"No, there weren't any angels involved." He smiled, watching how the glows from the firelight played across her little girl face. "But before the Night of The War, you could go places—fast food restaurants they called them. You could get hamburgers and chicken sandwiches and fish sandwiches. I always liked hamburger. But there aren't any animals now. When the Eden Project returns, they should bring back animals and after a while, there should be meat again. But it's a delicacy now."

He extended the jerked beef stick to her—Annie had processed some of the less appealing cuts of meat in the freezer into jerky. The darkness around them was cold, forbidding, but it was warm near the fire in the shelter of the rocks. He had given up on reaching the Place before dark, and had not wanted to come on it after the light was gone. He had worried over the fire, that guards from the Place might see it, or the cannibals. But the cannibals would be glutted and he had beaten them off once. And Madison had told him there were no guards at the Place.

She sat close beside him and he gnawed away a piece of the jerked beef. "Come on—I can't see where it's against your religion."

"The angels eat flesh?"

He avoided the remark. "This isn't flesh like you're thinking of. The people I call cannibals—the ones you call Them—they eat other people, the flesh of other people. This is the flesh of cattle. They were raised specifically to be eaten eventually. That was their function."

She licked her lips. She had eaten half the supply of dehydrated fruit and vegetables he had brought as trail food, the fruit and the vegetables from the garden. It had been only the last few years that they had actually gotten the fruit trees to bear, pollinating the trees themselves. She had eaten five of the fingers of cornbread Annie had sent with him. "I will try the flesh."

"That's a girl." Michael felt himself smile. He handed her the beef stick. He watched as gingerly she placed it near her mouth. "Think of it as meat—like hamburger or something."

"Hamburger," she repeated, touching the tip of her tongue to the rolled stick. Her tongue moved as rapidly as the tongue of a snake was supposed to move. He had read of snakes, seen thousands of them in a very famous movie his father had the videotape of. But the comparison to a snake was wrong somehow, he thought. Her tongue moved like the wings of a hummingbird. He remembered actually seeing one during the times he and his sister had been on the trail with their mother after the Night of The War. Her tongue moved like that.

He asked himself why he was watching her in such detail.

She placed the stick of beef in her mouth. Her nose wrinkled up a little and he laughed as she struggled to tear the bite she had taken from the stick.

She handed it back to him.

He watched as she held it in her mouth. "You don't have to eat it if you don't want to—I just wanted you to try it."

"It—is—is very tasty, Michael."

His arm was around her. He watched her mouth as she chewed, her throat, the movement there as she swallowed. "Why do you know so much about angels and archangels and so little about hamburger?" It was a stupid question, the way he put it, he realized.

She smiled, the firelight in her eyes, changing the shade of the blue there. "We read the Holy Bible. The Families—they read other things sometimes. But we read the Holy Bible and the Holy Bible is interpreted for us by the Ministers."

"Who are the Ministers?"

"The heads of the Families—men from each of the Families are the Ministers. It is always this way."

She shivered in his arm and he couldn't quite understand that because she was very healthy seeming and she was dressed more warmly than he, the sleeping bag she had used as a coat earlier when they'd walked now swathed around her

103

beside the fire.

He held her more closely against him.

"Do these Ministers—do they tell you about other things, besides the Bible?"

"Oh, yes, they tell us everything that we need to know."

"Have you ever wondered if there's maybe something you needed to know that they didn't tell you?"

"But the Ministers know best for us."

"You're beautiful, Madison."

She looked away. "You joke with me. I am not beautiful. Madame Elizabeth Cambridge is beautiful. Miss Genevieve Vandiver is beautiful. I am—"

"I said you're beautiful. May I kiss you?"

She raised her eyes, looking at him, the fire making shadows there one instant, the shadows gone the next.

"But you are an archangel and I am only a Madison."

"Then there shouldn't be anything wrong if I kiss you," Michael Rourke told her.

"I have never—I am not a breeder."

"A breeder—a breeder?"

"Only some from the Madisons can breed and I was not selected."

"To breed with whom—another Madison?"

"That is forbidden."

"To breed with whom, then?"

"With one of the Ministers, or someone appointed by them from the Families."

"And who do the male Madisons breed with?"

104

"After the first time—they may breed with any of the female breeders if the permission is given."

Michael Rourke felt a tightness in his throat he had never felt. "Breed with me, then."

Her eyes seemed suddenly so wide. "An archangel would not—"

"I told you, I'm not an archangel. I'm a man. And suddenly I want to breed with you very much. But we don't call it breeding. Although I guess that's what it is. I've never done it before either."

"If it is not breeding, then how would one say it then?"

He watched her face, her eyes—her lips. He touched his lips lightly to hers. She didn't move away. "It's called making love. And you're the first woman I ever kissed besides my mother or my sister or some relative years ago I can't remember."

"Michael." She whispered his name, saying nothing more.

His hands moved, almost independent of thought, under the sleeping bag that was around her, her arms folding around his neck. He felt her breath against his skin, his face.

She touched her lips to his cheek.

His hands found the buttons of his shirt that she wore beneath his sweater. There were snaps and he pulled at the shirt front, the snaps opening with a succession of tiny clicking sounds.

His hands felt things incredibly warm—burning. He had never touched a woman's breasts—until now. . . .

Chapter Twenty-Five

They camped at the site of what Rourke realized was his son's first camp. Being more experienced, they had made better time than Michael had. But then, Rourke thought, lying beside the fire, listening absently as Natalia and Paul talked, they had not been searching for something fallen from the sky. They were searching for a man and a machine. Only that.

He felt something against his cheeks—Natalia's hand—and he turned his eyes from the fire to stare at her, crouched, then dropping to her knees beside him, between his legs and the fire.

"Paul is going up into the rocks to keep watch. He said we don't need to relieve him. He can't sleep."

"He'll be like that for a few days—and then he'll really crash but good." Rourke smiled.

"He has left us alone."

"Subtle, isn't he?"

Natalia moved closer to him. "After we find Michael—then what?"

Rourke chewed down on the cigar. His daughter was an admirable cigar maker. Did her thoughtfulness make the taste all the better? he wondered. "You'll have to try one of these cigars and let me know what you think."

"I haven't had the urge—to smoke at least."

"Filthy habit." He smiled.

"I had five hundred years to break it. But some

things never change, do they, John?"

John Rourke folded his right arm around her shoulders, and she eased beside him, against him. "I'm sorry," he almost whispered.

She kissed him quickly on the mouth, and then she buried her head against his shoulder. In the darkness he couldn't tell, but he thought that she cried.

Chapter Twenty-Six

He sat at the small table that he used as a desk, reading the report.

There—far from where he was—it was wasteland, like it was wasteland everywhere.

Believing that they lived somewhere, that they lived somehow, had kept him alive. The substance whose chemical formula could not be reconstructed. He had stolen it in the last hours.

With a few of the others, he had used it.

He had survived.

They would have survived.

He felt this inside of him.

He stood up, throwing down the sheaf of papers that made the report, crossing from the smaller anteroom into his bedroom.

The girl was still tied to the bed, where he had left her tied.

There was little left of her.

She had been cleaned up—the bleeding stopped —and returned to him.

If the garbled grunts and noises she had made had been speech, this was lost to her.

She whimpered only, like an animal whimpered. When there had been animals.

But there was still pleasure in her for him.

Watching her stirred him and he began to undress, seeing it in her eyes, the fear he had put there, fear like flowers blossoming amid the bruises of her face, amid the welts and cuts. "You serve a great purpose," he told her. "There are women here, but I would not use them this way. But there is one woman. Perhaps after I find her, then perhaps after I do to her things I have never done even to you, perhaps then I will no longer care for this." And he smiled. "But," and he picked up the steel-cored rubber hose, watching the terror, hearing the insensate whimpers from her puffed and swollen lips, "until that time—" and he brought the steel-cored hose down hard across her face, the head snapping hard right. There was no movement, and the eyes only stared. There was no sound.

He sighed long, loudly, then threw down the steel-cored rubber hose.

He sat naked on the edge of the bed beside the dead female. He did what he had to do himself.

Chapter Twenty-Seven

Her body moved beneath him—violently was the only word he could think of to describe it. Her thighs burned at his flesh. Her eyes were closed, and he could see the lids flutter in the firelight. It was remarkable, he thought, how somehow something he had never done before seemed so natural, so perfectly natural. His body trembled—hers trembled beneath him, his arms aching as he held himself over her, her hands against the bare flesh of his behind. He could feel her nails as they dug into him, her body moving more violently now than it had.

Suddenly, he felt as though he would explode—and a part of him did and he sagged against her, his lips touching at her breasts, his head resting beside hers, his breath coming hard to him, the girl's body rising and falling hard against him, her lips moving, no words coming, then the words. "Michael. Michael. Michael." Over and over, she said his name.

Michael Rourke opened his eyes, very quickly. There was the sound of Madison breathing in the crook of his right arm, of the long night log crackling with fire. The sound of the wind, like a low whistle. But another sound in the darkness. He squinted to focus, studying the luminous black face of the Rolex Submariner. It was nearly four a.m.

The sound again, and Madison stirring beside

him, curling her naked body against his in the sleeping bag. Again he saw the wisdom of his father—a smaller gun that could perhaps be fired easily from inside a sleeping bag would be useful now. He had no such gun.

The Predator was beside him.

His left fist closed around the Pachmayr-gripped butt. Five rounds loaded, an empty chamber under the hammer. With a Ruger of modern design, there was no need for this precaution, but it was still advisable for added safety.

He lay perfectly still, waiting. Had it been before the holocaust, when the sky became flame, it could have been an animal. But there was no higher animal life.

His left thumb poised over the Predator's hammer.

Ready.

The sound of a twig breaking. Naked, Michael rolled from the sleeping bag, the hammer of the Predator jacking back, one of the cannibals, human skins layered over his body, a stone axe in both hands, was coming from beyond the fire. Michael twitched the Predator's trigger, the cannibal's body lurching with it, falling back into the flames, the human skins which covered the cannibal catching afire, the smell of human flesh burning on the wind, shrieks, more animal than human. Michael leveled the Predator, the hammer jacked back. He swallowed hard, pulling the trigger again, the sound like thunder, a tongue of bright orange flame licking from the muzzle, through the darkness.

Naked, shivering, he stood, waiting.

There was no sound from the cannibal, the fire consuming the flesh.

If any more of them were in the darkness beyond the firelight, they were not attacking.

He was aware of movement beside him and he swung the muzzle of the Predator toward the sound.

But it was Madison, naked like he was, staring at the fire.

He folded his right arm around her, drawing her close to him, her flesh against his flesh. "Michael —I love you," she whispered.

"Get dressed, we're sitting up the rest of the night. At dawn, we get out of here."

He looked down at her face. "Michael—"

"After we go to the Place, I want you to come back with me. To the Retreat. I want you to be with me. I guess that means I love you, too."

She buried her face against his chest, the fingers of her right hand knotting in the hairs there. "Yes, Michael."

Chapter Twenty-Eight

"There—there is the Place."

There had been no more of the cannibals. Michael Rourke assumed the man he had killed at four o'clock that morning—a little over four hours ago—had pursued them for a blood feud. He would never know, he realized. Beside him, clad in the improvised skirt, his shirt and sweater, the sleeping bag no longer needed as a coat about her shoulders because of the radical change in temperature after the rising of the sun, Madison pointed down the defile and into a verdant valley and beyond, to the far side of it.

"That cave?" Michael asked her.

"It is the entrance—the main entrance. I have always heard that there are other ways in and out known only to the Families. But the Place is there."

"How do you get in?" he asked her.

She looked up at him, her blue eyes pinpoints of color as the sun washed her pale face. "Michael would be better to think how we will get out of the Place. They will want to take me and return me to Them to appease Them. And you are an outsider—they will see that you too are one who goes."

He took her left hand in his right, saying, "Don't worry—I come from hardy stock," and with Madison beside him, Michael Rourke started down the defile and into the valley—toward the Place. . . .

The cave entrance was very close now, Michael not touching either hand to his firearms but ready. Suddenly, he asked Madison, "Why didn't you make some comment on my guns? If you thought I was an archangel and my knife was a sword."

"I saw the guns once. That is why I know you must be the Archangel Michael. No one can have guns but the Families. There is a very large room full of guns. Once, I was assisting the Cunninghams, cleaning the quarters of one of the Families. And at the end of this corridor, there was a big room and the doors were opened for just a minute. I looked up from my scrubbing through the doorway. I saw these things and one of the Cunninghams whispered to me what they were and that I should never mention them for any knowledge of guns was forbidden beyond the Ministers and the Families."

"Do they carry guns—the members of the Families, or the Ministers?"

"No—the electric stick."

"Cattle prods, I read of them," Michael noted half to himself. "They carry no guns?"

"No, I have never seen a gun beyond the confines of that room, and of course the guns that Michael himself uses. You are very skillful with these." She smiled.

He looked away from her. Staring down at the ground, they walked a moment. "My father is better."

"The father you speak of—he is Our Heavenly Father?"

Michael smiled, looking at her—smiled at her innocence. "No, he's my father and my sister's father."

"But he must be very wise, and know all things."

"Possibly," Michael told her. "When you come with me to the Retreat you'll meet him. It'll be time for the Awakening soon. I'll miss it. But perhaps Annie will wait."

"Annie—she is your sister."

"Right. And my father's name is John. My mother's name is Sarah. And we have a good friend named Paul and another good friend named Natalia. There were six of us. Now there'll be seven."

She touched at her abdomen as they stopped before the entrance to the cave. "Perhaps more than that," and she smiled.

Michael Rourke leaned down and kissed her lips quickly. Then he turned away and stared at the entrance to the Place. It was a cave, of natural rock, but had undergone much human engineering. It still bore scorch marks on the rock from the fires that had consumed all life—almost all, he corrected himself—five centuries ago.

He walked around behind her, then took her right hand in his left, the M-16 slung crossbody at his right side. He had packed the crossdraw holster for the Predator in his pack, the Predator concealed under his shirt behind his left hipbone. The A.G. Russell Sting IA was clipped inside his sock on the inside of his left calf.

By nature, he reflected, he was not a trusting soul.

They entered the cave, the cave entrance broad

114

and high, the walls narrowing as the cave penetrated the rock of the mountain itself.

"I am frightened," Madison whispered, but her voice was picked up by the walls, echoed, amplified, reverberating around them like a thousand loud whispers.

He did not answer, still moving. He saw no entrance yet, no entrance into the mountain.

He stopped, leaning down to her, his lips touching at her right ear as he whispered, "Where's the entrance?"

"I do not know—one is taken for sacrifice to Them blindfolded and the blindfold is removed when one is outside."

"What do you do when you normally go outside?"

"We never venture out—because of Them."

Michael Rourke rose to his full height. He was as tall as his father and had been since he was just shy of seventeen. He looked behind them— nothing. Ahead, there was nothing. His palms sweated and he loosed her hand for a moment to wipe his left palm against his blue-jeaned thigh. He took her hand again and started ahead, holding the pistol grip of the M-16 now in his bunched right fist, his thumb poised near the selector. If these people had guns but never used them, he rationalized, a modest display of firepower might avert any danger.

They kept moving.

Nothing ahead. He looked back. Nothing behind.

They kept moving, his fist tightening on the M-16, twenty-nine rounds in the magazine, one round already chambered.

"I am frightened," she whispered again, and again the echoing, the thousand whispers, only more distorted now. The construction of the cave—how much was man-made he was uncertain—formed a natural whispering gallery, a natural security system for the slightest sound. Gradually, he had been becoming more aware of their reverberating footfalls. If he did fire a burst from the M-16, aside from the potential for ricochet, there would be a deafening noise.

He kept moving.

His mind raced, calculating the possibilities for a hidden entrance. There were shackles built into the side wall—to secure the sacrifices. He had read the books his father had read before constructing the main entrance to the Retreat. Was the doorway to this place opened by a system of weights and counterbalances? It would have to be, he reasoned, for otherwise, how could the structure be secured against unwanted entrance when the owners or users were all away. It was obvious to him, that what he was about to enter—however he was about to enter it—was a survival retreat, constructed before the Night of The War. But how had the people survived?

Then a thought chilled him. The constant level of population. It had to be as he had surmised—genocide, institutionalized genocide with victims who were willing to go.

There were no large rocks visible, like there were outside the Retreat.

Where was? . . . He heard the sound, wheeled toward it, shielding Madison behind him, swinging the M-16 forward taut against its black web sling, a panel opening out of the living rock, a human face, and then another and another, men, three of them, immaculately tailored three-piece business suits, but in bizarre contrast to this each of the men wore bedroom slippers. In their hands were swagger-stick-shaped objects, perhaps eighteen inches in length. The cattle prods, Michael surmised.

"All right—hold it. I'm coming as a friend. I don't mean you any harm. You know what this is," and he gestured with the assault rifle. "But the girl isn't to be touched. You expelled her and she's with me now." He felt her hands against his shoulder blades.

One of the three men—a man on each side of him—smiled. "You are not from the Place. You are not from Them. Others live then."

"Others live." Michael nodded, lowering the muzzle of the M-16 slightly. "My family, two of our friends. And there was an aircraft. I didn't find the wreckage, but I found the pilot's parachute. And the pilot was slaughtered by the ones you call Them. I didn't have any chance to search through his things and find out where he came from. But there must be others alive as well, and somewhere technology has survived. The world can rebuild and grow and there'll be no need for all of you to live here underground and—"

"Michael!" It began as a word and ended as a scream, Michael wheeling, the pressure of Madison's hands against his back suddenly gone. Madison was being dragged toward the opposite wall by more of the men in immaculately tailored three-piece business suits and bedroom slippers, cattle prods held to her flesh as she screamed incomprehensibly.

Michael moved the M-16 forward, opening his mouth to shout, to order them—then the pain. At first he could locate the origins. The small of his back, the center of the back of his neck—the word he remembered abstractly was "nape"—and where his right arm joined his shoulder.

The M-16 fell from his hand, on its sling, his body twitching uncontrollably, the pain flooding him now, Madison screaming, "Michael!" the pain, Michael Rourke falling to his knees, feeling something he had never felt before, everything in his field of vision fuzzy suddenly and green and a cold sweat on his skin, the feeling of nausea in his stomach. He sagged forward, rolling on the rock floor of the cave, trying to make his right hand respond and find the pistol grip of the M-16. Through the green wave washing over him he saw Madison being dragged through the opening in the rock wall on the opposite side of the cave.

She screamed again, and he heard it as his eyes closed and his head struck against the rock and the darkness flooded his consciousness. "Michael!"

Chapter Twenty-Nine

In the intervening day, she had seen her mother four times. Four times her mother left the room her father had built for he and his wife to share, entered the bathroom and then returned to the room.

She sat at her sewing machine, her left foot on the pedal that gave the machine its electrical power, her left hand feeding the material beneath the needle, her right hand giving added tension to the thread, working the hand wheel on the side of the machine as she hemmed the blue floral print skirt she had been making for the last several months. She did most of her sewing by hand—it consumed more time and the supply of fabric was not inexhaustible, but she wanted this finished now so she could wear it when Paul returned.

Annie looked up from the machine, her mother standing in front of her. Sarah Rourke wore a man's shirt—Michael's or their father's. It was blue chambray and there were at least three dozen of them. Her mother's hands were inside the pockets of a pair of blue jeans. On her feet she wore no shoes or socks. "Let's talk, Ann."

Ann—no one called her that. "I can make us some tea—you'll like it."

"You make the tea, I'll make some lunch. I'm hungry."

"I can—"

"I know you can—but I'll make it."

Annie flicked off the light on the sewing machine and stood up . . .

"He likes you—I don't mean Paul. I mean, that's obvious, but I mean your father." Sarah Rourke was stirring sliced potatoes in a frying pan. She had taken meat from the freezers. "Why'd you look at me so oddly when I took out the meat?"

"There isn't very much meat, Momma, and Michael and I always saved it for special occasions. I was thinking I'd make a roast when Daddy and Paul and Natalia got back with Michael—like a special occasion. It'll be the first time the whole family—"

"The whole family," her mother repeated. "Yes, just the six of us. A father and mother who collectively aren't ten years older than their children's ages combined. The four of us, plus Paul and good old Natalia, the KGB major. Paul's very nice. I'm surprised at the friendship between Paul and your father. Your father never really made friends. He raised you to mate with Paul."

"I know that—but that's not why I feel the way I do, and if Paul feels the same way, that isn't why for him either."

"You're probably right. And he raised Michael for Natalia—that's obvious."

"He was trying to—"

"Did your father ever ask me?"

"The potatoes will burn."

"No, they won't. I've been doing this a hell of a lot longer than you have. He never asked me. I took the sleep expecting to wake up at the same

120

time everyone else awakened. Not to wake up twenty years after my children did, not to find them already grown just so Natalia and Paul wouldn't be forced to marry or whatever it is people can do when there are only six people alive on earth." She cut off the burner and began shifting the potatoes into a serving bowl, then took a potholder and checked the oven for the meat. "Your father never cheated on me—never once. I'm sure of that. But he cheated me, cheated me more than he ever could have if he'd cheated on me."

"But we—"

Sarah turned around, her eyes staring, harder than Annie had ever seen them. "If you marry Paul Rubenstein, if you and Paul have children—how would you feel closing your eyes and seeing them as children, then opening your eyes the next instant of consciousness and seeing them fully grown, missing all the years in the middle. How would you feel? Who told you what to expect when you were growing up—from your body, I mean? Who taught you everything you didn't teach yourself?"

"Well, Daddy did, but—"

Sarah Rourke whispered, "You finish dinner— I'm not hungry."

"But . . ."

Annie watched her mother walk away, to the bedroom, but Sarah Rourke didn't look back.

It wasn't as Annie had planned it—it wasn't that way at all.

121

Chapter Thirty

John Rourke dismounted the Harley. By taking a route through the mountains that he and Paul Rubenstein had learned of by accident in the weeks following the Night of The War, he had saved two days of travel. Natalia dismounted as well. All about them were telltale signs of a camp. A fragmentary motorcycle tread. Burned wood from a fire, and signs of a fire being meticulously put out.

"He's been here, all right," Paul volunteered.

Rourke looked at the younger man, but only nodded.

Rourke studied the partial tread print, looking up from it, ahead, then taking off in a long-strided jog, his eyes scanning the ground through the dark-lensed aviator-style sunglasses, a cigar, unlit, clamped between his teeth in the left corner of his mouth.

Another tire impression—he stopped running, dropping to his knees to examine it. "Natalia, bring up my bike. Paul, cut an arc of about one hundred eighty degrees about a hundred yards ahead of me—ninety degrees on each side of where I'm at now."

"Tracks—right."

Rourke stood to his full height, taking the Zippo in his right hand, flipping it in his hand, not opening it, not really intending to light the cigar as yet.

He glanced skyward, then confirmed the time with his watch. Three hours of daylight remained. If he could second guess Michael's route as he had earlier, they might be able to cut through the mountains again in such a way as to intercept Michael's next campsite before total darkness.

He was trying to cut the gap of time between them. Rourke felt a smile cross his lips—he realized, chronologically less than a decade older than his son, that he'd already done that.

"Ready."

He looked at Natalia, then looked away as he mounted the machine.

Chapter Thirty-One

He had lost count of the hours, and realized he had lost count of the days. The cattle prods they had used—his body ached as he moved. He had been away from the Retreat—how many days? He shook his head to clear it, dismissing the question until a later time.

Cautiously, before assessing his surroundings, he felt under his shirt beside his left hipbone. The revolver—it was still there. As he sat upright, his back screaming at him with the pain, he felt inside his left sock—the A.G. Russell knife was still there.

Michael Rourke looked up, unable to keep the smile that he felt coming from etching across his face. He was alive. He was armed.

He assessed his surroundings as, with difficulty, he stood. An ordinary-seeming room, but there were no windows. A door—it seemed made of metal. He approached it, about to touch it to confirm—but he stepped back. With their penchant for electricity, he was uncertain. He looked upward—there seemed to be no observation cameras in evidence, no microphones. Perhaps the room—almost a khaki color for walls, ceiling and the linoleum-covered floor—was just that, a room. Nothing more.

Perhaps too they expected him to walk out of it.

He licked his lips, reaching down to his sock, removing the Sting IA. Gently, he tossed the all-steel knife against the door. It clattered to the floor. There was no evidence of electricity. He picked up the knife, stepping back from the door again.

He threw the knife—gently, again—this time the knife bouncing against the doorknob, sparks of electricity sputtering into the air.

Michael Rourke stepped back.

After a long moment, he picked up his knife. Quickly, he resheathed it, concealing it, then dropped to the floor. He began to unlace his right combat boot. His father had told him the story of the last seconds before fire had engulfed the planet, of the climb to the top of the mountain which held the Retreat, of using the double magazine pouch like a heavy leather glove to insulate his hand. The boot off now, Michael placed his right hand inside it, flexing the leather so he could grip with it.

He thought suddenly of Madison. If they had killed her, he would kill them—it was very simple, very logical. He remembered, as they had lain together after discovering each other, she had asked him what the white flakes which fell from the sky had been and he had explained the crystalline structures which when examined were never at all like any other. He had explained that some had theorized that perhaps as they fell, the flakes may indeed have fallen into certain patterns and that the infinite variety came about from the constant melting and refreezing they underwent as they passed through different temperature layers, or fell upon the warm ground to partially melt and then refreeze. She had stopped him, laughing, telling him that she thought they made his hair and his eyebrows look pretty. What did one call them, she had asked. Snow, he had told her. And she had repeated the word several times.

He approached the doorknob—he'd free her somehow, he told himself.

But as he reached for the doorknob, the knob sparked, then turned.

Michael Rourke drew back, ready to go for his gun.

One of the men in a three-piece business suit stepped into the doorway from the corridor which Michael could partially see beyond him. "You are to come with us. The Ministers wish to see you. We can use the electric sticks again if you resist."

Smiling, he dropped to the floor. "Just let me get my boot on, guys."

Chapter Thirty-Two

They had traveled for most of the night, gotten six hours of rest and then moved on before daylight. More of the shortcuts through the mountains and John Rourke estimated they had saved perhaps as much as two days of travel time compared to Michael's route. He was exploring. They were searching, a more single-minded pursuit, Rourke had told Paul Rubenstein.

Natalia beside him now, Paul on foot moving through the woods beyond the clearing, looking for signs, John Rourke stood, staring at the remains of a fire. It was not one of Michael's fires. Littered around the clearing, most prominently near the fire, were human bones.

Natalia, her voice low, whisperlike, said, "Cannibals."

"Michael parked his bike and moved through the clearing on foot—he went right to them."

"Human beings, John—he was looking for more of his own kind. That's why he left the Retreat. But there was no sign of him returning to the bike."

"He headed after them," Rourke added somberly.

He looked at her, Natalia's eyes looking into his. "What would you have done?"

He laughed a little. "Gone after them—just like Michael—under the circumstances."

"You told me you taught him to be very good with a gun. And Annie—she said he practiced regularly."

"Yeah, but all he took with him was one assault rifle and those two single-actions he liked. And two knives. That means, in a firefight, just one viable weapon. Those handguns are super for what they were built for—hunting, backup in the game fields, silhouette shooting. Not for combat. And anyway, he's on his own."

"They've been on their own for fifteen years. Annie told us Michael would leave the Retreat sometimes to go off exploring."

"Never this long. And anyway—he's not just some guy. He's my son. I'm worried. Cannibals," and he dropped into a crouch beside an almost neatly stacked pile of human ribs, the bones spotless.

"John—oh, shit—John!"

Rourke was up, running, Natalia ahead of him, both of the Metalife Custom L-Frames which bore the American Eagle symbols on the barrel flats coming into her hands, Rourke snatching the Python from the full flap holster at his hip.

He slowed his run, Natalia stopped already beside Paul Rubenstein, Paul's hands shaking, the sling for the MP-40 subgun rattling.

Rourke walked over to stand between them. In the bushes was a human head, the smell of the rotting tissue strong. The eyebrows were reddish tinged; the scalp and the skin above the middle of the forehead had been peeled away.

"Cannibals?"

Rourke looked at Rubenstein. "Yeah," he almost whispered.

Chapter Thirty-Three

Michael Rourke glanced at his Rolex—the date had changed, ever closer to Christmas and the time set for the Awakening. He had been unconscious from the electrical shocks overnight. They—the three men in the business suits—had let him stop in a bathroom. He had urinated and defecated, and washed his face and hands, noticing the stubble on his cheeks as he studied his face momentarily in the mirror. He looked identical to the sleeping visage of his father in the cryogenic chamber.

His three business-suited guards with their high-powered cattle prods walked with him as he moved down the corridor now, a large, double-doored room at one end. Was it the armory Madison had spoken of? he wondered. He made a mental note to investigate it.

The corridor made a left bend and at the far end where the corridor stopped there were two ornate wooden doors, like something one might expect forming the doorway of a conference room.

"You will go inside and await the Ministers," the one who had spoken earlier told him, opening the right hand door. Michael noticed the door handle. It looked to be made of gold and ornately figured.

"What about you guys?" Michael asked.

"The Ministers will see you." The man held open the door. Michael walked through. The room was lit with conventional-looking ceiling fixtures, but bulbs rather than the fluorescent tubes which would have been more in keeping with the room, he thought.

A long, expensive-looking conference table dominated the center of the room, space to sit perhaps two dozen people: mentally, subconsciously, he began counting the chairs—twenty-eight, one larger chair at each end. At the far end, before the larger of the two largest chairs, were two candles, but neither candle was lit. He was alone in the room as far as he could ascertain.

He looked to the walls on each side of the room, and then to the wall on the far side of the room. Murals, crudely painted, very stylized, at once modern, primitive and yet almost juvenile, filled the walls. His mouth was suddenly dry. It was the Night of The War, cities burning, missiles raining down from the skies. He had seen none of this where they had taken shelter that night in the barn opposite their house. But he had heard the stories around the campfires of the Resistance, remembered the stories his father had told of overflying the cities that night as they were systematically turned to ashes. Both flanking walls depicted this horror and he looked away from it, to a horror that had been worse, one he had seen, did remember, could never forget. It was the last sunrise, the holocaust, the end of the world, the sky aflame, lightning bolts crackling through the skies, ball lightning rolling across the ground, bodies on fire—death.

"These have meaning to you, young man?"

He turned around. The conference room doors closed. There were seven men, all in immaculately tailored business suits and red fabric bedroom slippers, their ages varying from younger than his own to what he judged might be late seventies. The same voice—the oldest one of them was slightly bent, balding to the point where a wispy fringe of white crowned the sides of his head, the light from the overhead bulbs gleaming dully off his head. "You remember this from stories?"

"I saw this—with my own eyes—the holocaust, when the skies caught fire."

"Heresy," one of the others murmured.

"But I—I am very old, and I saw none of this."

"It's a long story—but we utilized a special scientific process, for cryogenic sleep."

"What is this cryo—this—"

"Cryogenic sleep."

"We?"

"My father and mother, my sister, our two friends. The six of us. We'd thought we were the only people left alive."

"You wear shoes of leather, boy."

Michael Rourke looked at his feet, and then at their own. "They were made five centuries ago but well-cared for."

The old one who had done all of the speaking except for the word "heresy" laughed. "Five-hundred-year-old shoes on a five-hundred-year-old man who looks to be perhaps thirty years old—"

"I turn thirty next month—but what I say is true. Who are you?" Michael asked.

"I am the man who will decide your fate, along with my six associates."

Michael Rourke licked his lips. "What is the Place?"

"It is our home." The old one smiled, almost laughing.

"Who are Them?"

"Outcasts, young man—they are outcasts."

"From where?"

"From the Place, outcasts sent from the Place over the course of the last several decades."

"Where is Madison?"

"She who was Madison fifteen, until it was decided she would be one who goes?"

"Yes—the one you call Madison fifteen."

"She was called that, but she is called nothing now."

Michael started for the old one, but the man raised his hands, palms outward and he smiled. "For the moment, this girl is quite safe and quite well. You will see her again, I assure you."

"I came here in peace. I saved Madison from the ones you call Them. I forced her to bring me here. I search for people of my own kind. Do you have aircraft?"

"Machines which fly? Of course not."

"Someone does—there was a crash. I couldn't find the wreckage. But the pilot—I found his parachute. And he was being killed by Them. That's how I came to rescue Madison. I only came for knowledge—not for violence. Believe that."

"You came with the guns. This one is called a handgun, I think?"

"Yes—a handgun."

"And the other one—it is called?"

"An automatic rifle." He said nothing of his knowledge of the arsenal which he had gained from Madison.

"We have many such implements, but they are never used. They are dusted, they are given oil—"

"Where do you get oil from?"

"Peanuts which we grow. We distill an oil to a specific formula given to us over the ages."

"Why do you keep guns if you don't have a use for them?"

"They were used by our progenitors and have religious value to us and this is why we preserve them. But we do not need to make shoot with them."

"To make shoot," Michael repeated. "Right." He wished he smoked like his father had. "Listen —I came in peace. Give me my guns, give me the girl—I'll leave with her."

"Your guns have been added to ours. There they shall remain."

"Fine—gimme the girl, then. You keep the guns."

"We will not give you the girl and allow you to leave, as you say, because then you might tell others of this place."

"There are no others," Michael told him. "Except the cannibals. No others. Whoever came in that plane, I don't know where he came from, and even if I did, I wouldn't tell him about you—if you let us go in peace."

"Have you no curiosity, young man—about us? We have about you. Tell us your story and we shall tell you ours."

"I'd love to, but maybe some other time. I'll bring Madison back to visit or something."

The old one laughed. "A sense of humor—my goodness. How refreshing."

"Thanks. Now—"

"No. We shall recount our story. We have never before had the chance," and the old man started from the doors and crossed near Michael. Michael felt the temptation to reach out and throttle the man, use him as a wedge to get past the others and find Madison and escape. The old man just looked at him. "If you attack me, it will gain you nothing. It is nearly time that I become one who goes. Harming me, or the threat of harming me will not gain your freedom from here. But you must be curious."

"All right, I'm curious—tell me."

133

The old man smiled and Michael noticed that a cataract partially covered his left eye. "Do you have doctors?" Michael asked as the old man shuffled toward the head of the table.

"We have healers but an attempt to prolong the time before one goes is forbidden."

"Super—just let people die."

"One does not do this thing you say, young man—one goes." The old man was easing into the largest chair, before the two candles.

"You go outside and get torn apart by those cannibals like you sent Madison. You die—pure and simple."

The old man laughed.

The other six men moved about the room, one lighting the two candles at the head of the conference table, another opening a wall safe behind an inset wood carving in the back wall, the carving out of place amid the mural of the end of the world. From the safe, another of the six assisting him, he withdrew two books. One was leather-bound and the size of a Bible or unabridged dictionary, the other smaller, leatherbound as well, but the size of a diary. "What are those?" Michael asked.

The old man looked up, "Why, the holy books, of course."

"The large book—it's a Bible, right? But the other one—it looks like a diary."

"It is the last book, written by our progenitors and it is locked and shall remain so for all time."

"You revere a book as holy and yet you have no

134

way of knowing what it contains?"

The old man smiled indulgently again. With great effort, he stood, one of the others assisting him. He reached to his vest pocket, extracting from it on the end of what appeared to be a gold chain a small key. "As head of the counsel of the Ministers, I carry the key. It is my badge of office. The key will unlock the second holy book, but the key is given to us to test our faith and will never be used as it has never been used."

"If it's a diary, it probably tells something you should know—it's not wrong to pry into the writings of someone who's gone if it will help you to stay alive in a situation like this."

"You are a most peculiar young man." The old man smiled again as he sat. "The second holy book is five centuries old. And to stay alive as you put it is not a problem to us. And what situation? A situation requiring desperate measures? I think you misunderstand me. We thrive here. We have happiness here. There is no desire to alter this at all. So, then, why should sacrilege be committed and the second holy book be opened? But perhaps you will better understand after I recount our story."

"Go ahead." Michael nodded.

"Be seated—there, in the far chair from me."

Michael looked at the second largest of the two large chairs. He moved the chair as he approached it—no wires, nothing out of the ordinary. He sat down, placing his hands on the polished table before him. "So, tell me your story, if that's what

135

you want."

"Yes—it is what we want, young man."

"My name is Michael—Michael Rourke."

"The Place," the old man began, seemingly oblivious to Michael having given his name, "was built more than five centuries ago, and at great expense and labor. It was the fashion, as the story has been passed down to us, for persons to plan to survive warfare among the nations of men, or disease, or economic trials. And so, the Place was built. And it was staffed. Because of the guns and because of the expense of the fixtures here in the Place, security persons were used to protect the Place from outsiders. The war between the great nation of the United Statesof and the evil nation of Commie took place—"

"It's the United States of America, not United Statesof, and the nation of Commie—it was the Soviet Union. The Soviet Union was run by a Communist government, and sometimes Communists were called Commies. You're telling me an oral tradition, aren't you?"

The old man resumed, as though, Michael realized, nothing had been said. "The war between the United Statesof and the Commie began, but our very wise progenitors foresaw this time of grief and took shelter in the Place and the Place sustained their every need. Time passed, and the great fires came from the heavens and consumed the earth as it was prophesied in the Holy Bible. But our progenitors in their wisdom had become the Chosen of God and it was His decree that the

136

Place and our progenitors remain unscathed. And when the fires consumed all that was evil and had purged the land and the waters and the air, only the progenitors and their servants remained. Yet the servants were evil, consumed by jealousy of the wisdom of the progenitors and sought to hurl out the progenitors from the Place, but they were not successful, and as punishment for this blasphemy, the servants were put out. It was decreed that the number of one hundred persons should not be exceeded over seven days. And so, it is the descendants of the servants who are set out into the evil of hell which surrounds us, and consumed by Them, the ones who eat the flesh."

The old one looked up, smiling—he seemed somehow pleased. Perhaps that he had remembered it all, Michael conjectured. "What you're saying is that you practice institutionalized genocide on persons you consider racial inferiors. And that the ones you threw out eventually became able to survive, by cannibalism, and now you continue the practice to feed them."

"You eat flesh—this can be seen from the things you wear on your feet."

"I eat meat, but the meat of cattle and other animals raised for human consumption. But since the holocaust, there has been no fresh meat so we eat very little meat at all."

"By his own words, he admits his origin, sir," one of the younger business-suited men said to the old one.

"From hell thou art and to hell thou shalt

return—both you and the girl."

Michael stood up. "Wonderful—you're letting us leave. You think outside is hell—this is hell. Never going outside, killing people to keep the population in perfect balance. You're all crazy."

"They shall be bound and set aside to be consumed by Them."

Michael's right hand flashed under his shirt, the button there already open, his fist closing around the butt of the Predator. "Uh-uh, guys." Michael stabbed the .44 forward, aiming it toward the opposite end of the table, his right thumb jacking back the hammer. "You're plain out of luck. I'm finding Madison and my guns and I'm gettin' the hell out of here."

"See how he defiles the Conference Room!" It was the one who had proclaimed Michael as guilty.

"See how I defile your face when I blow your fuckin' brains out," Michael whispered, his voice low. "My advice—open that diary, read it. Maybe you were meant to read it, and if you weren't, then maybe you should anyway."

Michael started toward the door, backing up, glancing once behind him—the doors were still closed. He assumed the three guys with the cattle prods would be outside—but the gun would even the odds substantially. "Where do you keep the girl?"

The old one smiled, but said nothing.

Michael nodded. "OK, I'll find her—then we'll be out of your hair, you'll pardon the expression," he added, the light reflecting from the top of the man's head.

Behind him, he felt the doors. He reached for the handle. . . .

"Not gold," he rasped, the electricity surging through him, the Customized Ruger falling from his right fist, not discharging, his body shaking, trembling, pain. "No!" He sagged forward, the blackness coming, but his hand unable to release the door handle.

Chapter Thirty-Four

The door opened, and she shrank back into the corner, three of the ones from the Families, two of them with gloves on, dragging Michael. His body shook, his eyelids fluttered as they rested his body on the floor, walking from the room without looking at her, the third one closing the door.

She left her corner, on her knees, moving to be beside Michael, her right hand gently touching at him—she felt the mild shock his body still carried, her hand drawing back, cradled in the palm of her left hand on the faded gray skirt of her uniform.

"Michael—Michael, answer me. Michael—please—Michael!"

His eyelids fluttered again, but did not open.

His right hand—it twitched. The flesh on the

inside of his fingers—it was black and burned.

She could not touch him until the electrical current left his body—she had seen what the electrical current could do before.

On her knees, still, she rocked her behind back against her heels, her body swaying, her hands still in her lap, her calves cold-feeling against the bare floor. It was a holding room. She knew where she would go. She had been placed in a holding room once before—when the Families had selected her as one who goes. To Them.

She felt tears in her eyes, felt them dribble down her cheeks.

Her archangel.

Michael.

He was human after all.

And in her heart, the thing Michael had talked about as love—she felt it stronger for him now as she knelt at his side.

"Michael . . ."

Chapter Thirty-Five

The wind of the slip stream was cold against his face, but every few moments he would feel the warmth of Natalia's breath against the back of his neck, her body close against his as they rode searching for Michael's trail lost in the rocks an hour earlier. They had split up, Paul running a search pattern to the south, Rourke and Natalia searching to the north. All they had uncovered was another campfire of the cannibals and more—but vastly less this time than before—of their ghastly leavings: human bones.

"John."

He turned his face right, to speak over his right shoulder. "What is it?"

"I think I saw movement in the rocks—above us and to the left."

He nodded. "I saw it a little while ago. I think we've got company. Our cannibal friends."

"What about Paul?"

"He'll be all right—so'll we. It's Michael I'm worried about." He glanced up into the rocks—a furtive blur of motion, then nothing.

He slowed the Harley, stopping it at the close of a wide arc, cutting the engine. "What are you doing?"

"I'm going up there—gonna catch a cannibal. Get him to talk."

"John!"

"They won't come down here after us. I'll go up after them."

He felt her hands leave his waist where they had rested as they had driven. She dismounted the Harley, Rourke dismounting as well. He un-zipped his coat, pulling off his gloves, folding them after straightening them, putting them in his bomber jacket's left outside patch pocket. He took a cigar from the inside pocket of his jacket, the end

141

already cut away as was his habit, putting the cigar in the left corner of his mouth, clamping it tight between his teeth. "You back me up from down here—and listen for any gunfire from Paul. He should be on the other side of the rocks. If it sounds like he's getting into trouble, you double back and I'll cut across the top."

"You don't know how many of them there could be, John."

"They don't have guns," he told her, his voice low. "At least I don't think they do. But I do. Anyway, maybe we can just talk," and he smiled.

"Don't—I mean—just because it is Michael—don't—"

"I won't," Rourke whispered, leaning toward her, kissing her cheek lightly.

He pushed the CAR-15 farther back on its sling so it was across his back, then started toward the rocks.

Chapter Thirty-Six

He would find his son—there was no question of it, he knew. He kept moving, across the bare rock face, moving upward slowly, his rifle swaying away from his back, then swaying against it. He had seen no more movement above.

Rourke looked back once, below him, Natalia,

her hands on her hips, standing beside the jet-black Harley, black like the black of the jumpsuit she wore—her battle gear—black like the boots she wore. Black like the color of her hair—but her hair was only almost black for there was no true black in nature he knew.

Rourke kept moving.

Sarah. Natalia. But now the task was to find Michael. He had laughed at Annie when she had awakened them early from the Sleep, laughed at her premonition, her dream. But the cannibals—he had not anticipated this. How any men could have survived on the surface was incomprehensible to him.

There were mysteries in this new earth. If the Eden Project returned, there would soon be machining capabilities. Perhaps an aircraft could be built. As it was, the Harley's engine would power a light biplane more than adequately.

He kept moving, reaching up with his right hand, then bringing his left leg up, then his left hand, then his right leg, repeating the sequence as he climbed higher, the edge of the higher rocks more clearly discernible now. He kept moving.

His left hand reached out, and with his left leg he thrust himself up against the meager purchase below the height of the rocks, half falling forward onto the rock surface.

Rourke pushed himself up and rolled away from the edge, flat on his back for a moment, resting from the exertion in the thin air, setting himself as bait to the cannibals, for them to attack.

No one came.

After several minutes, he rolled onto his abdomen, then pushed himself up, standing to his full height. He walked back toward the edge, waving down at Natalia. She waved back. Michael would be more used to the thinner air. In time, he too would become used to it.

He turned away from the edge, staring across the flat expanse of the height of the rocks. He reached into his Levi's pocket, finding his lighter. He smoked less and less—in the thin air, intentionally damaging his lung capacity was insane. But he lit his cigar now, rolling the Zippo's striking wheel under his thumb, plunging the tip of the cigar into the wind-dancing blue-yellow flame, flicking the cowling shut with an audible click.

It was the stillness. No sudden engine noise betraying a Soviet patrol or a Brigand biker gang, no gunshots from off in the distance, no one. Nothing.

The Earth was a dead place.

And he supposed the cannibals were its new-found scavengers.

He moved ahead, dragging easily on the cigar, his breathing still rapid from the exertion of the climb, his rifle across his back again rather than at his side as he had placed it before making the final assault on the top.

He wanted to look like easy prey.

Rourke kept walking.

Could these people talk? Could they understand?

Where had they come from?

If these cannibals lived, however few in number, others lived too, he knew.

He kept walking. "Hey—I want to talk," he called.

No answer. "Do you speak English?"

No answer. *"Habla Espanol?"*

No answer. *"Parlez-vous Francais?"* he laughed. He could ask the same question in German, in Russian, perhaps another language or two if he racked his brain for the right combination of words.

"I didn't come to harm you," he shouted. "I came searching for one who looks like me."

And Rourke stopped. "One who looks like me," he whispered. If Michael had met the cannibals and fought them off, they would think he— Rourke—was his own son. If Michael had died—a shiver ran along his spine. They would think he was Michael's ghost.

He gambled on life, smiling to himself—it had been the one commodity on which he had always gambled.

He reached down to the holster at his hip, slowly withdrawing the Python. It was big, shiny—close enough in appearance to Michael's handguns, at least to the untutored eye. Slowly, Rourke raised the gun over his head. Then slowly again, he dropped into a crouch, flexing his knees, setting the pistol on the ground.

The CAR-15—it too looked near enough to Michael's M-16. He slipped the sling over his head and set the rifle down, the safety off but the chamber empty. Michael carried two handguns, and Rourke reached under his jacket for the Detonics in the double Alessi rig. He snapped the pistol from the leather, setting it down beside the Colt revolver and the CAR-15. There was still one under his right armpit. The little Detonics Combat Master .45 looked nothing like Michael's smaller .44 Magnum Predator—but again, Rourke thought: To the untutored eye.

And a knife. He gambled Michael had likely had only the one knife visible—the big Gerber. Rourke unsheathed the black-handled Gerber MkII and set it down beside his guns.

He stood. "There," he shouted. "No weapons!"

He stepped back one step, then a second step, then a third. His palms sweated.

There were boulder-sized rocks scattered all along the top of the mountain, and from behind one of these now stepped a man. He was clad in human skins, a woman's head of hair dangling obscenely near his crotch. In his right hand was something Rourke considered at least slightly more mundane—a stone axe, the handle perhaps two feet long, a massive flat rock laced to it with what Rourke surmised would likely be human hair woven into rope. "Do you speak English?" Rourke called out.

The cannibal's face seamed with something half between a smile and a snarl, his body bending slightly forward as his left hand joined his right on the axe. From behind another rock, another of the cannibals, then from behind still another rock still a third, the second two armed like the first, each with a massive stone axe. Rourke owned one, a Cherokee Indian stone axe. But he had never fought with it—as these men, barely men, seemed intent to do. The first one—with the woman's hair near his crotch—started forward in a loping, crouching walk.

Rourke didn't move away. "I didn't come to kill you—probably. I want my son. He looks like me—just like me."

The first cannibal was coming closer, the other two hanging back slightly. Rourke swallowed hard—the reason for the man's loping walk, he realized, was a bullet wound, the left side of the man's body sagging, leaves plastered over the left shoulder, dried blood there as well. The wind shifted, and Rourke could smell it—the wound was suppurating. "I'm a healer—for information on my son, I'll heal your wound."

The cannibal kept coming, raising the stone axe now to swing.

The only other person alive—possibly—who could have shot the man would have been Michael. For that reason, as the cannibal moved toward him now, Rourke would not reach for the second Detonics pistol, or the Black Chrome Sting IA.

The axe started the downstroke, Rourke sidestepping quickly, wheeling half right, his left leg snapping up and out, a double Tae Kwon Do kick to the left side of the cannibal's head, the cannibal

147

staggering, not falling. The other two were coming now, screaming something so guttural Rourke couldn't even be certain the screams were not words, threats, the second cannibal closing. Rourke wheeled again, sidestepping as the stone axe cleaved the air where his head had been, a high sweeping forward kick with his right leg, then wheeling, the same high sweeping kick again, but this time the left leg, this time connecting against the jaw of the second cannibal, the axe flying from his hands. Rourke stepped in, the heel of his left hand hammering up and out, impacting the base of the cannibal's jaw, his right hand punching forward, the middle knuckles finding the solar plexus—the human skin the cannibal wore over his own was cold, damp to the touch.

The cannibal sagged back, Rourke's left knee smashing up, hammering into the testicles, but Rourke feeling no squish as the cannibal doubled forward, Rourke sidestepping to avoid the cannibal's breath. The body fell.

Rourke wheeled, the third cannibal charging, the first man up as well, grabbing his stone axe.

Rourke spun one hundred eighty degrees left, back-kicking the cannibal once, then again in the chest, as Rourke's right foot settled back to the ground. Rourke's right fist backhanded the man across the center of the face, the nose shattering, blood spraying on the wind, Rourke wheeling right one hundred eighty degrees, a left hook to the cannibal's jaw, then backhanding the cannibal across the face again on the backswing.

The third cannibal was too close. Rourke threw himself down to the rock surface, rolling against the cannibal's shins, the axe flying, the man's body sailing over him.

Rourke rolled onto his back, both legs coming up, snapping outward and down, Rourke up, to his feet, the second cannibal coming again. Rourke's right fist snapped outward into the center of the face once, then again, then still again, the cannibal sagging, falling.

Rourke wheeled left, the third cannibal on his feet again, coming, the axe in a giant swing laterally, Rourke wheeling, sidestepping. Rourke reached down to the rock surface, snatching up one of the fallen stone axes—the stones were wound to the wooden shaft with what Rourke recognized as dried and cured human intestines.

Rourke swung the axe upward, blocking the lateral thrust of the cannibal's axe, Rourke's right foot snapping forward and up, into the jaw of the cannibal, Rourke backstepping. The axe heads locked, dragging the man forward and down as teeth spit from the cannibal's cracked and bleeding lips.

The cannibal rolled forward, Rourke sidestepping, half wheeling right, Rourke's left foot snaking out, a fast double kick to the side of the head—he might be killing the man, Rourke realized. The man still moved, another double kick and there was no movement.

The sound of feet against stone, Rourke wheeling. The first man, the one who bore the gunshot wound, he was coming, charging, blood covering his face and chest, the axe high over his head.

There was no choice—Rourke swung the axe in his own hands, cleaving the stone head into the right chest cavity of the charging cannibal. The cannibal's body rocked with it, the cannibal recovering, swinging the axe in a horizontal chop. Rourke blocked it with his own borrowed axe, pulling his opponent off balance. The cannibal swung the axe again, Rourke dodging back, dodging again on the backswing, Rourke's own axe coming up, powering down, impacting the crown of the skull, a crunching, splitting sound, blood spraying in a pink cloud, then gray—the gray of human brain. The cannibal's body fell backward, impacting the stone, bouncing, blood spraying upward again, the body rocking, the arms sagging, spread-eagling, still.

The second cannibal, moving quickly now, reaching out for Rourke's rifle. Rourke didn't know if the man could use it. He couldn't gamble. Rourke leaned out on his left leg, taking a half step as he wheeled ninety degrees left, his right leg fully extended forward, his hands and arms bringing the axe down diagonally, impacting the left side of the neck, the stone axehead locking in the chest cavity, a hideous scream, then a cloud of blood, then the smell of sphincter muscles relaxing, human excrement pouring from between the cannibal's legs, the head hanging by a thread of flesh, flopping across the right side of the chest cavity as the body fell away.

Rourke let go of the axe handle.

He stood there a moment. The remaining cannibal was unmoving, still on the rocks where Rourke had kicked him repeatedly in the head to put him down. The eyes were open. Rourke assumed death.

He reached down for his weapons—there was gunfire, the short, light bursts from Paul Rubenstein's Schmeisser, a familiar sound he hadn't heard for five hundred years.

Stuffing the Metalifed and Mag-Na-Ported Python into its holster, the CAR-15 and the Gerber in his left fist, Rourke balled his right fist around the Pachmayr gripped butt of the Detonics pistol—Rubenstein needed help. Three shots was the signal he had found something. There was another burst of subgunfire.

Much more than three shots—Paul was in trouble.

Rourke was already scanning the far side of the rocks for a way down.

Chapter Thirty-Seven

One moment he had been alone, inspecting what might have been tracks, then the next, sounds of branches breaking, of footfalls. He had wheeled, fired, fired again and again, cutting

151

down at least six of them, falling back as the others regrouped behind low rocks.

He stood beside his machine—there was no need for cover. They were armed only with stone axes. His stomach churned—they had worn human skins for clothing, some of them with the facial hair or the hair from the head still intact, one wearing on the center of his chest what appeared to be a skinned human face—eyelids and lips still evident.

The magazine in the Schmeisser he judged as more than half empty—too startled to count his shots, something he had taught himself to do, something he had made second nature. But the sight of them—he shivered, stabbing the partially spent magazine into his trouser belt, taking a fresh thirty-two round stick for the Schmeisser and ramming it up the well.

Paul Rubenstein shifted the Schmeisser to his left hand for an instant, drawing the battered Browning High Power from the ballistic nylon tanker-style shoulder rig in which he carried it. The pistol in his belt, butt pointing left for access with his left hand, he took the subgun into his right fist again, steadying it with his left, waiting.

Rourke had used the expression once—a drug-store stand.

Both 9mms ready, he was ready.

And the cannibals were coming now, raising from their positions behind the rocks.

He fired a controlled three-round burst from the Schmeisser—but the cannibals didn't hide, didn't run, didn't fall back.

His fists locked to his weapon, he watched it, almost as if it were in slow motion, the cannibals, their stone axes swinging wildly over their heads, running to meet him, screams and shouts he couldn't understand issuing from their mouths.

He shifted the muzzle of the Schmeisser left, then started to fire, hosing them, cutting them down, stone axes launching toward him as the men who had wielded them fell, but more of the cannibals coming, like a human wave, he thought. He zigzagged the muzzle of the Schmeisser again and again, putting more of them down, more of them still coming.

And the Schmeisser was empty.

Paul Rubenstein let the subgun fall to his side on its sling, no time to reload it, finding the butt of the High Power with his left hand, drawing it from his belt, jacking back the hammer with his left thumb, the chamber already loaded, thrusting the pistol outward, firing once, killing, firing again—a head shot—and the body falling, firing again, a hand loosing a stone axe, the body rolling back and down. Firing again, a stone axe flying skyward, a body spinning out, tumbling to the ground. But some of the cannibals he had already shot, with the subgun, now with the High Power, they were rising—coming.

As if they were not perhaps human, as if they were unkillable.

His right hand found the Gerber MkII fighting knife John had given him. Rubenstein drew the knife, holding it ready in his right fist like a short sword, still firing the High Power, bodies falling as the stone-axe-armed cannibals closed.

There was a shout from behind him. "Paul—hold on!" The roar of a motorcycle engine.

"Natalia," he whispered, the High Power empty in his left fist, no time to reload, his right hand punching out, burying the Gerber into the chest of one of the cannibals—through the skin of some anonymous dead woman which the cannibal wore—burying the steel up to the hilt.

The High Power—he crashed it down against the forehead of one of them like a skull crasher, the cannibal's body sagging back.

The roar of the bike again as a stone axe swung down toward him and he raised his left arm to block the blow however he could. A burst of automatic weapons fire—an M-16, a sound he knew well. The cannibal holding the axe crumpled, Paul sidestepping as the axe fell toward him without a hand behind it. In an instant he realized that a hand did still grip the axe, but the hand was no longer part of an arm. A scream—Rubenstein had the Gerber free and stabbed it into the chest of the cannibal with the severed hand.

The bike—a blur of motion and color, the blackness of Natalia's clothes, the bike impacting at the knot of the cannibals surrounding him, bodies flying, screams, more bursts of assault rifle fire as Rubenstein hacked into the human wall closing on him with the blade of the Gerber and the butt of his pistol.

More assault rifle fire—then it choked off. "Natalia!" He screamed the word so loudly his throat ached with her name.

The thunder of a heavy caliber revolver, then again and again, bodies peeling back from him.

Natalia was suddenly there, firing her gleaming Metalife Custom L-Frames point blank into faces and torsos, the bodies of the cannibals nearest him falling away.

A clicking sound—her guns were empty, he realized.

Then another sound—click, click, click, then a scream. The Bali-Song, the gleaming steel catching the sunlight, flashing across faces and chests and hands and arms, screams of the cannibals.

She was beside him now, and suddenly they were back to back, only their knives—

"John should be getting here," he heard her pant.

A cannibal came at him with a stone axe upraised—no way to block it, he realized.

He started to thrust the Gerber forward.

A sound then—a sound like no other, the flat booming of a .45, again and again and again, bodies peeling back. More of the shots from .45s, rapid succession, then throttled off, then the thunderlike sound of a heavy caliber revolver again—it would be John Rourke's Python. Rubenstein sidestepped, stabbing the Gerber into the chest of the stone axe wielder.

Natalia spun beside him, hacking with her Bali-Song against flesh, screams, the booming of the

155

Python again and again and again.

Rourke's face, Rourke's body shouldering through, a knife in each hand. Natalia screamed, "We're winning!"

Rubenstein's right arm ached as he worked the knife, cutting, hacking, killing until he lost count.

After a long time Paul Rubenstein lowered his knife—because there was no one left to fight. Dead. Departed.

He would have fallen to his knees to rest but there was no spot near him that wasn't littered with all or part of one of the cannibals.

He heard Rourke talking as he closed his eyes. "Only the most fit, the most strong among them would have survived, the very toughest. We'd better get out of here after we check the skins they're wearing—that one of them isn't Michael's." And Rubenstein shivered but he opened his eyes so he could look for some fragment that would look like John's face—which was Michael's face—and he prayed he couldn't find such a thing, not find it at all.

And he reloaded his weapons in case they would come back and there would be more killing to do.

Chapter Thirty-Eight

There had been no one alive to interrogate,

Natalia reflected, realizing at once that the thought was horribly cold-blooded. But she had interrogated prisoners before—and she hoped she would never again. As she hugged her face against Rourke's back, the leather of his battered brown bomber jacket rough against her cheek, but good-feeling to her, she wondered almost absently what she would have been like had she never joined the KGB as a young girl fresh from the Polytechnic and fresh from studies of classical ballet.

She had met Karamatsov at the Chicago School in the Soviet Union. It was called the Chicago School, she had always been told, because the type of English taught there, practiced there, used unflinchingly there, was Middle Western urban English, the most accent-free. She had learned the advanced techniques of her then-new craft there. And she had met Vladmir Karamatsov there, the experienced field agent, the senior officer, the hero who daily had braved the hateful Americans in his fight to preserve the people of the Soviet Union. After marrying him, she had learned that he was a lie, and that so much of what she had been taught in school, so much of what she had been taught in the various levels of her KGB training had been a lie.

And John Rourke, the man whose body she hugged herself to as the Harley vibrated beneath them, speeding across the bumpy and rocky trails through the mountains—John, at her uncle's urging, had killed Vladmir after Vladmir had nearly killed her in a fit of rage, violated her

157

humanity to the point where she had fought him in order to survive.

And she had fallen in love. With John Rourke. And now his wife seemed to despise him, or at least his actions, and the action had been for her, she realized. He could say he had planned for the survival of the race, that six adults, three mating pairs would be far greater guarantee of survival than only one. He could explain the logic. When he and Sarah someday died, the children would have been perhaps faced with incest or the extinction of the human race.

And he would not have two wives—it was not his way. And Paul—Rourke had wanted to provide for Paul's happiness as well. Rourke had allowed his children to age to adulthood.

And now, with only the most fragmentary clue, they searched for Rourke's son. For Michael.

John had theorized that Michael, having encountered the cannibals, would have pursued the cannibals rather than the mysterious light he had seen in the sky, and so they had left the due northwesterly course they had followed ever since leaving the Retreat, backtracking the cannibal's movements by their hideous trails of cookfires and human bones.

That they ate their own weakened or sick was obvious, but where had they come from? They could not have survived on the surface after the sky had taken flame.

Where?

She shuddered—less from the wind of the slip

stream than from the fear they would find out.

Chapter Thirty-Nine

They had found tracks of Michael's bike, then lost them again, doubling back.

Dismounted, they stood now just inside the treeline, Rubenstein pulling away the withered brush. "It's the bike you took from the Brigands after they attacked the airplane, John."

Rourke looked at the younger man, then back to the blue Harley Davidson Low Rider.

"Check her to see if she'll run—that gives us a bike for each of us until we find him."

"Why would he have gone on foot?" Natalia asked.

Rourke looked at her—really seeing her for the first time in days, the surreal blueness of her eyes, the near blackness of her hair, the thing intangible inside her that made it so obvious to him that she loved him. "Michael would have been getting close to something—maybe a concentration of the cannibals that he'd followed. The engine noise would have frightened them off and apparently he wanted to observe them. So he left the bike. No pack, no other gear. Either he got in trouble and couldn't get back for it or he's still following them close."

"Then what should we do, John—if he's that close to them maybe? What about our bikes?"

Rourke glanced to Rubenstein for a moment, then back to Natalia. "There'd be a several day lead on us most likely—if we start getting close to something, we'll play it by ear. But on foot we'd be forced to travel too slowly. We can cover in an hour more territory than he could have covered in a day. We could find him by morning, maybe," and Rourke looked skyward, the sun low, yellow-orange on the horizon.

"We can go on in the dark for a time at least," Natalia announced.

Rourke only nodded.

His eyes were searching the ground and he moved now back from the bike and toward the partial clearing beyond the trees. It was guesswork only, he realized—no footprints would be visible on the hard ground. And the snow that had come and gone so quickly would have helped further to eradicate them.

He wondered absently if it would snow for Christmas? Would he be home for Christmas?

Did he really have a home?

And he looked up from his search of the ground for a footprint he knew would not be there, feeling Natalia's hand at his shoulder.

And he saw in her eyes what he had thought he no longer had.

Chapter Forty

The lights had been off when he had awakened, the room as dark as a starless and moonless night, but he had felt her beside him in the darkness, heard her whispered murmurings, her tears that they would each soon be one who goes. And he had tried, not yet able to move, to explain death to her as he understood it. And that her understanding of her religion was not all as it should be. And he had held her—and she had cried again that if she carried his baby inside her that it too would die and Michael Rourke had not known what to say to her.

It had been hours by the luminous black face of his Rolex—their only light in the darkened room—before he had felt he could move sufficiently well. But he had unbuttoned the front of the dress she wore—she had told him it was gray and a worker's uniform, hours before he had touched his hands to her flesh, his right hand paining him but the softness of her body making the pain less something of which he was aware.

He had slipped between her legs, to do again what they had done before—how long ago?

Only a night.

Her body had moved with him, beneath him, surrounding him, and she had shuddered against him as he had shuddered against her. The clinical side of him reflected upon something he had read about the possibilities of simultaneous orgasm.

But they had felt it together and that, he knew inside himself, was what had mattered.

He was his father's son, he knew, but in the darkness there holding Madison's burning warmth close against him, he realized he was not his father. What little remembrances of his father's relationship with his mother were remaining to him—it seemed somehow different. And perhaps he carried in him some of his mother as well, the emotions which he remembered. Tears, smiles, gentle songs in the night.

Michael Rourke smiled. He had discovered himself—he wondered if most people discovered themselves too late as had he.

There was still the knife—still the little knife in his sock. He could pick the knife up from inside his emptied boot where it was now, use the knife when they came for them at dawn. He assumed it would be dawn, no desire to ask Madison, to make her remember.

He could kill some of them, with the knife, with the martial arts skills his father had taught him, kill some of them and before they got him, kill Madison, to spare her the torment of being skinned alive by the cannibals, to spare her that.

Michael held her more closely. One thing his father had taught him well—to never give up.

And very suddenly too, as he now felt he understood himself, he felt that he understood his father's torment—the woman Natalia. If there were anything to forgive his father, he forgave it.

Life was to be lived. Michael touched his lips to

Madison's forehead, felt her stir against him, felt her hands searching for his face, her lips finding his. To be lived, he thought—as long as it could be.

Chapter Forty-One

He had decided to wait—they were not bound, merely blindfolded. There had been no ropes in evidence, no manacles—only the prods and the admonition not to try to escape.

He could feel the shifting in temperatures as they moved, hear sounds he recognized from having read of them—an air lock. The Place was hermetically sealed—it was how it had survived the holocaust.

But the price for survival had been too high.

A second door opened and he was urged through with the prods, but they were not activated.

Voices—he had counted six as, blindfolded, they had first been led into the corridor.

Six men—he could kill six men, then perhaps escape with Madison into the hills beyond the Place. He could fight off the cannibals again.

"Wait here," one of the voices from the blackness called.

A clicking sound.

Madison had told him before the business-suited men had come for them. There were shackles built into the wall where she had been left for the ones she called Them. He had seen them when entering. The shackles required no key but needed to be opened with two hands and the shackles were so placed as to keep the victim spread-eagled against the wall.

It would be in the farthest reach of the cave, nearest the mouth, he knew—he could feel the coolness of the air on his flesh.

"Come with me. Do not try to resist," one of the anonymous voices called from the darkness.

Michael Rourke had never liked orders, he reflected.

His right hand—toward the voice in the darkness. His left hand—toward the blindfold which covered his eyes.

The right hand—it found flesh, twisting, ripping.

The left hand found cloth—twisting, ripping.

He blinked his eyes tight against the misty light—it was dawn, the sun rising beyond the mouth of the cave, shafts of yellow light like hands across the cave floor as he ripped the flesh of his enemy toward him, his left hand punching forward into the face of the business-suited guard as the man raised the cattle prod in his defense.

The nose—Michael shattered it. Wheeling, back-kicking, his heel found the groin, driving the body back and away from him, his right hand reaching down to find the cattle prod, the other five of them coming for him, closing, Madison, the blindfold pulled from her eyes, screaming, "Look out, Michael!"

Michael sidestepped right, ducking, wheeling— there had been a seventh man. He should have realized—the cattle prod hammered down toward him, but his right hand and left hand held the wooden prod and he rammed his prod back, into the abdomen of the seventh man, doubling him forward. Michael loosed the prod with his left hand, his right still holding the prod, snapping out in a wide arc, across the nose of the nearest of the five men coming for him, the man falling back.

Another prod slicing the air toward him, his right arm going up, blocking the prod with his prod, his body half wheeling left, his right foot snapping up and out, into the abdomen of his opponent, then his right arm snapping back, hammering the prod across the man's face, knocking him down.

Three remained, two of them starting for him, their prods held like sabers, the ends of the tips glowing hot orange with the electrical pain they could cause.

Michael started toward them, hacking the air before their faces with the prod, one of them falling back, Michael wheeling to the second, feigning a strike with the prod, the man dodging, Michael wheeling half right, a double Tae Kwon Do kick to the chest.

The second man—he was driving fast, the prod in both hands to block a blow from the hand or arm. Michael drew his feet together, jumping, upward, his right leg flashing outward, the flat of his combat-booted right foot impacting the prod at the center, the prod splintering, breaking, the man holding it falling backward, losing his balance, regaining it as Michael dropped, his knees springing, taking the fall, the prod still in his own right hand out, aimed toward the face of the man.

The man edged back, Michael thrusting the prod forward, Michael sweeping the prod left to right, the man's head bobbing back, Michael wheeling half right, a double Tae Kwon Do kick, the man dodging as Michael had known he would, Michael holding the prod in both hands now, ramming it outward in a straight line for the man's Adam's apple, a scream, the smell of burning flesh as the edge of the prod impacted skin, the man caving in, falling back—dead, Michael realized.

The last men—he was going through the air lock—to lock them out, to leave them . . . for Them. Sounds, guttural, barely human if human at all, from the mouth of the cave.

Michael looked back once, shouting to Madison. "Run—for me—hurry!" The ones she called Them were coming.

Michael's right hand found the coat of the escaping guard, jerking back, the man lunging with his cattle prod, Michael's prod fallen, Michael's left hand snapping forward, the heel aimed for the base of the chin. The man ducked—Michael's hand impacting the base of the nose, breaking it, driving it up and through the ethmoid bone into the brain.

The air lock door was jammed half open, but the body sagged, Michael throwing his weight against the door—but it closed, a clicking sound as it locked.

Michael turned. The mouth of the cave—dozens of the cannibals, their stone axes held high to strike.

Beside him—Madison hugged at his left arm.

Michael reached down to the cattle prod, holding it now in his right balled fist.

His left hand—he found the knife hidden on his left leg.

He clenched the steel in his left hand.

"Stay behind me—won't let them get you."

Trapped, the air lock door closed, the cannibals filling the mouth of the cave in greater numbers by the minute. Michael Rourke stood his ground.

"Michael—we—"

"Just stay behind me," he told her. "Behind me."

He could see the lust for blood in the eyes of the cannibals as they approached.

Chapter Forty-Two

The panel of rock had slid back into position—

it was as if the door into the Place had never existed, Michael Rourke thought.

He felt Madison's hands behind him, touching gently at his neck where his shirt stopped. "Michael—kill me."

It was the first time she had used the word. "Make me die."

He looked at her—no longer did she think in terms of "goes"—and as he looked at her, he whispered, "If it comes to that, I won't let them have you. I love you."

A tear, a solitary tear, left the corner of her right eye and started to journey across her cheek. Then her eyes were rimmed with them.

Michael Rourke looked away.

The cannibals, the ones she called Them, the spawn, he realized, of the rigid population control inside the Place, were closing. One of them could have been her father—Madison's—or her brother. He had seen no cannibal women, which meant there was somewhere a village.

Women, children—children who would grow to become this, he thought.

Survival.

There were some prices too high—the cannibals paid such a price, the ones in the Place paid it as well. Inhumanity had spawned inhumanity.

He had left one of the bodies on the ground, the man still alive—for an instant. A stone axe cleaved into the skull. A dozen of the cannibals fell on the body, snarling, growling, snapping their teeth at each other, dismembering the body, hacking it to pieces, Madison screaming, "Michael!"

One of them had the man's left leg over his shoulder, the leg dripping blood.

Another of the cattle-prod-armed guards—this one already dead, his body fallen on by another group of the cannibals, torn, the flesh ripped, one of the cannibals biting into the raw flesh of a human thigh dismembered from the hip joint and from the calf.

The other bodies—Michael edged back with Madison pressed behind him as the other bodies were one after another set upon, torn, some of the cannibals lapping blood from their victims.

One of the cannibals—a human ear being chewed half outside the right corner of his mouth—turned from his meal, staring.

He gestured toward Michael, Michael watching.

There was a grunting sound—another of the cannibals turned, blood dripping from both corners of his mouth.

More of the cannibals turned toward them now, some of their axes catching in the sunlight as it grew to fill the cave, red glistening from them, the wetness of human blood.

A cannibal started for him—slowly, his axe raised.

As the cannibal lunged, Michael stabbed the cattle prod forward, the hot end impacting the cannibal's right eye. There was a scream, more hideous sounding then anything Michael had ever heard and the cannibal fell back, whimpering.

A memory, he wondered, of the pain of the

electric sticks?

Michael brandished the prod, ready, waiting—waiting for what he knew was inevitable.

Three cannibals now—the first one crawling off, holding his hand to his eye—three now came toward Michael. Their axes were raised high.

A sound—deafening, like rolls of thunder, then a woman's voice. "Hold it—or we will kill you all!"

The sound of a submachine gun—he remembered it from his childhood. A man's voice—not his father's. "She means it—so do I."

The cannibals turned one by one, slowly, parting slightly, in two waves, a corridor forming from the rear of the cave, where Michael stood ready to defend Madison, to the mouth of the cave.

Backlit, a shadow because of the sunlight behind him, Michael recognized the man at the center of the mouth of the cave, a gleaming Detonics .45 automatic in each fist.

The voice—a voice he had not heard for fifteen years, a voice almost identical to his own, a voice. "If you understand English, let them pass. Let them come to us."

There was no answer from the two waves of the cannibals which flanked him, flanked Madison. Michael waited.

His father's voice again. "Michael, come ahead—slowly. Keep the girl beside you, not behind you. Slow—don't do anything sudden."

He answered his father. "All right, Dad."

"They don't speak English—I'm sure of that by

now. But they remember enough to understand. When you're close enough, I'll toss you a gun—loaded and ready to go. They won't let you out of here."

Michael looked behind him, to Madison. She whispered, "He is your father—you are in his image."

Michael felt himself smile. "Stay beside me—and if we get out of here alive, still stay beside me."

"Always," she whispered.

He leaned toward her, touching his lips to her forehead.

Then he looked back toward the mouth of the cave. The black jumpsuited woman holding the M-16 was Natalia Anastasia Tiemerovna, Major, KGB—he knew her face well, like he knew the face of the man at the other side of the cave—the high forehead and thinning hair, but no glasses. He smiled—Annie had been right. Paul Rubenstein wouldn't need them.

"Major Tiemerovna," Michael called. "Good to see you after all these years."

"Michael, you are your father's mirror image."

"I know that." Michael nodded, holding Madison's body against him, his left arm around her slender shoulders, the knife in his left fist still.

He walked forward, calling, "Mr. Rubenstein—or is it Uncle Paul?"

"Paul's fine. Chronologically you're older than I am now."

"This is Madison—she doesn't have any other name. But she will—I'm going to marry her. Or

171

whatever it is you do when the people outside are cannibals and the people inside are religious fanatics who use genocide for population control."

John Rourke, from the mouth of the cave, his voice so low Michael could barely hear it, whispered, "Madison—daughter."

"We can't leave here. The people inside—we have to stop them," Michael called, walking slowly, cannibals on each side of them now, closing behind them as he looked into Madison's eyes.

"All right, son—if you feel we should," his father answered. "Just keep coming. Steady. Even."

"What are you gonna toss me?"

"My CAR-15—remember, it's not an M-16. One of these days maybe I'll change it around."

"All right. Thirty-round stick?"

"Thirty-round stick," his father answered, the cannibals closing tighter around them.

"If it's a choice, Dad—"

"I know. Madison—I promise," his father answered.

"There will be no choice," Natalia's voice echoed through the cave. He liked the sound of it—firm yet feminine, warm yet with something his father had told him was once termed "cool" to it. "We will all get out of here alive."

"You're lovely. I see why my father feels like he does for you. He told me once, before he took the Sleep, so I'd care for you if something went wrong

172

and you awakened and he didn't. He loves you."

"You have a big mouth," his father laughed from the front of the cave.

"I'm your son," Michael called back, ready with the cattle prod—to thrust it into his first attacker to free his right hand for the CAR-15.

He saw his father move, slowly, stabbing one of the pistols into his belt, all but his father's face clearly visible now in the growing light inside the cave.

A silhouette—a scoped assault rifle, the stock a different shape from that of an M-16, the barrel seeming shorter.

"What happened to your guns?"

"Inside. They have an arsenal in there and they don't do anything but clean it—don't even know how to use guns."

The cannibals were tightening around them.

"Michael, you and Madison stop moving. I'm coming to you."

"John!"

His father didn't answer Natalia. He began to walk, the CAR-15 in his right hand, almost casually it seemed, his arm hanging down at his right side. In his left hand, one of the Detonics pistols.

Michael stopped, holding Madison tighter against him, some of the cannibals starting to reach out to touch at her or at him.

"She can go between us—Madison can," his father said, his voice low, like a whisper.

He could see his father's face in greater resolu-

173

tion now—the dark-lensed aviator-style sunglasses, the cigar clamped tight in his teeth, the teeth perfectly even, perfectly white. "Can she use weapons, son?"

"I will try," Madison stammered from beside him.

"Good girl." His father nodded, the right corner of his mouth raising in what looked like a half smile.

The cigar wasn't lit.

John Rourke stopped walking, less than a yard separating them. Slowly, he reached out his right arm, extending it to nearly full length, the CAR-15 inches from Michael's chest. "Give Madison that stick—don't drop it. Make your play when I do. Natalia and Paul'll back us up."

Michael pushed the cattle prod into Madison's right hand. Her hand was trembling.

Michael raised his right hand to the rifle, closing his fist onto the pistol grip, inserting his trigger finger through the guard, his thumb finding the selector, verifying that it was set to fire.

He lowered the rifle to his right side.

He watched his father.

John Rourke reached slowly into a side pocket of his Levi's, his right hand reappearing, the Zippo lighter in it.

John Rourke flicked back the cowling.

Michael Rourke could hear the sound of the striking wheel being rolled under his father's right thumb.

Flame—blue-yellow, steady.

The cannibals shrank back, grunts, sounds, hisses. "You didn't tell me you were a specialist in mob psychology." Michael smiled.

"You pick things up, son." His father stabbed the tip of the cigar into the blue-yellow flame and the flame flickered now, smoke exiting his father's nostrils as his father drew his head back.

The lighter—the cowling flicked closed.

The right hand moved to the right side pocket, the thumb hooking in the pocket for an instant, then the lighter disappearing. "Count to three."

"One," Michael almost whispered.

"Two," his father murmured.

Michael's father's right hand flashed to the Detonics pistol at his belt.

Together, father and son. "Three."

Chapter Forty-Three

Natalia repeated the word under her breath in the instant it was said. "Three."

The muzzle of the M-16 raised as the thought passed through her, the assault rifle responding as though it were one with her will, firing, short three-round bursts, high, over the heads of John Rourke and Michael Rourke and the girl named Madison, into the cannibals behind them.

Father and son stood back to back, the girl

between them, the CAR-15 making fire from Michael's hands, in John's clenched fists in the twin Detonics stainless pistols, the heavy thudding sounds they made, bodies falling.

The rattle of Paul Rubenstein's MP-40, the shrieking sounds of ricochets, the reverberating of the gunfire and the screams of the dying in the confines of the cave mouth.

Rourke's .45s were empty, she realized, not seeing him shift guns, but hearing as the dull thudding sounds were replaced with the sharper, explosive cracks of the Python. Her own M-16 empty—as it fell to her side on its sling, both her hands found the butts of the Metalife Custom L-Frames, Rourke's .357 Magnum still firing as her own .357s began to discharge.

A cannibal fell as he lunged for her, then another and another.

Her revolvers were empty and there was no more gunfire except for the light cracks of Paul's Browning High Power.

The Bali-Song—from her hip pocket into her hand, the lock working off under her thumb's pressure, the handle half flicking out, back, out, the knife open, the Wee-Hawk blade slicing cannibal flesh, a carotid artery spraying blood as the body fell.

Michael Rourke. John Rourke.

She could see both men now, Madison still between them, each of the Rourke men wielding one of the stone axes, hacking, chopping at their common enemies, the screams, the shouted snarls

176

that perhaps were curses in the grunted language of the cannibals, death surrounding her as she slashed and hacked with the Bali-Song.

On the far side of the cave, the cracks of Paul Rubenstein's pistol had stopped—he would be using his blade now, too.

She could see the Rourke men—ahead. She fought toward them.

Chapter Forty-Four

He heard the girl Madison screaming behind him. John Rourke wheeled, three men with axes closing on his son. Rourke shoved the girl aside, hacking outward with a stone axe, killing the cannibal nearest her, stepping forward between Michael and the three cannibals, his own axe swinging outward against the face of the farthest cannibal, impacting the head of the second. The axe of the third was on a downswing, Rourke sidestepping, his son moving—a blur of motion, the axe of the third man gone, the face crushed.

Madison—her scream again. Rourke wheeled toward her. She was hacking outward with the cattle prod, the smell of burning flesh on the air for an instant, the cannibal falling back. The thought crossed John Rourke's mind—they'd make a good Rourke of her.

Michael—his axe chopped downward, against the head of the man Madison had struck with the cattle prod.

Rourke brought his axe through in a wide arc, five of the cannibals falling back, the impact then against his left shoulder. He stumbled, the axe falling from his hands, his upper body numbed for an instant.

Michael stepped past him, the axe in Michael's hands flailing outward.

Rourke's left arm was numb, but his right hand found the butt of the Gerber MkII in the belt sheath and drew the blade, thrusting into the attackers with it, withdrawing, thrusting, withdrawing, a swiping hack across an exposed artery. He wheeled quickly as the blood sprayed.

Natalia—she was beside him, fighting, her Bali-Song flashing in the sunlight that now filled the cave, red blood dripping from the blade.

Paul—his fighting knife wrenched free of a body.

And it had stopped—Rourke's right hand held the Gerber, poised, ready, but the cannibals who still stood were withdrawing, backing out of the cave or running in fear.

There was a clicking sound—John Rourke knew it well, the sound of a fresh magazine going up the well of Rubenstein's Schmeisser. "Leave 'em, Paul—let 'em withdraw."

"All right, but in case they come back we'll be ready again."

Rourke only nodded.

He glanced at Natalia—she was wiping her blade clean on a bandanna handkerchief. "Here—use this for your knife," and she passed it to him. Rourke nodded. "Paul and I can take care of getting the bikes down here—Paul can ride them down one at a time and I can cover him."

"Takes too much time—cover him for the third bike, then each of you ride the last two down—"

"You found my bike!"

He looked at his son. "Yeah, we found your bike," and John Rourke laughed.

Chapter Forty-Five

That the cannibals would return was not something Rourke thought debatable—it was obvious. Michael and Madison had shown Natalia the location of one of the door panels in the rock wall of the cave and Natalia, Paul helping her, was already at work to open it. She had laughed. "All that KGB training—I was always very good at breaking into things."

John Rourke stood at the mouth of the cave, his son beside him, Madison with Paul and Natalia.

"I guess I fucked things up."

Rourke looked at his son. "Welcome to the club."

"What do you mean?"

"Ahh," and he sighed loudly, long. "Your mother—she's angry. More angry than I've ever seen her. Because of what I did—using the cryogenic chambers to let you and your sister reach maturity while the rest of us slept."

"It was the only practical thing."

"Don't let your mother hear you say that."

"She'll get over it."

"I don't think so. Maybe it'll be good in a way—like you said that maybe you'd gotten Madison pregnant. A grandchild—but at her age," and John Rourke felt himself smile. There was no sign of the enemy but they had already proven they were good at using natural cover. They could be ready to attack again, Rourke realized. "No—maybe a grandchild will help her feel better about herself, but it won't make her feel better about me."

"You mean—"

"I don't know what I mean," John Rourke answered, looking at his son. It was like staring into a mirror—Michael stood well above six feet, a full shock of dark brown hair, brown eyes, the prominent jaw, but there were fewer lines in his face and unlike John Rourke, not yet a trace of gray. "I thought we might have lost you. But I'm embarrassed—I should have known you could take care of yourself."

"It was touch and go there for a while," his son laughed. "I'm glad you and Paul—and Natalia—I'm glad you all showed up when you did." And Michael seemed to clear his throat, his voice odd-sounding as he almost whispered. "I was going to kill Madison if I had to."

"I know that."

"You would have done the same, wouldn't you?"

"Yeah, I would have—and I wouldn't have liked it any better. This thing, this thing with your mother and with me, well—"

"I figured we could go exploring together—see what's out there, you know, and—"

"You're gonna have a family—"

"That never stopped you," Michael answered.

Rourke looked away and smiled. "No, it never stopped me. Maybe it should have, son—maybe it should have."

"If Madison is carrying a child, well, there'll still be time. Before the child comes, after."

"What—leave the girls at home? You and me—and Paul—"

"Well, sure. Paul, too—he's your partner and—"

"Best friend I ever had. You are too, but you're my son. So that allows me to have two best friends. But whatever happens," and Rourke lit another cigar. "Well, don't get into this thing between your mother and me—it wouldn't be right for her to think I'd turned you or Annie against her. I never wanted—"

"Doesn't she realize why you did it—I mean, I know. You set things up so Natalia and I would, ahh—"

"Am I that transparent?" Rourke laughed.

"Yes, you are—yes."

Rourke nodded. "I guess I am. But it didn't work, did it?"

"You were willing to give up Natalia for your love for Momma."

"You mean I was willing to give up one woman I love for the other woman I love—that doesn't say a whole hell of a lot for me, does it?"

"But all that time you searched for us and you never—"

"No," Rourke laughed. "I wanted to—God, did I want to. But as long as there was a chance your mother was alive . . ."

"I don't—"

"Your mother and I," Rourke said softly, exhaling a cloud of the gray cigar smoke, watching it dissipate on the air, then staring at the glowing tip and the ashes as they formed there. "We fell in love with each other—we're still in love. At least I am. And she is, too—yeah. But, ahh, we were never—well, we were never really friends. I knew this couple once—the guy was a writer. He and his wife—you never saw two people so much in love. But they were buddies, pals—friends. The friendship and the love coexisted. I, ahh, your mother and I—we never—" and Rourke inhaled hard on the cigar.

"What about you and Natalia? Are you friends?"

Rourke looked at his son. "We're friends. It's your mother's play. I'll do what she wants."

"What about Natalia if, ahh—"

"Ahh, what?" Rourke smiled. "I don't know. I

182

woke up from that second period of cryogenic sleep, ya know? Annie had this dream—said it's only the second time in her life she remembered a dream, and that she saw you in danger. We oughta listen to that kid more. But I woke up," Rourke sighed, exhaling the cigar smoke again, watching it again as the wind caught it and made it dissipate. "Your mother was heartsick—and I decided I'd never try playing God again. I mean I didn't try this last time—I just tried to do what was right, what was best for all of us. Well, I did that, ya know," and Rourke snorted loudly, his sinuses bothering him suddenly. "I did what—what I thought and, well, shit," and he inhaled on the cigar again and opened his eyes wide against the wind.

And he felt his son's hand on his shoulder.

Chapter Forty-Six

Annie Rourke hitched up her skirt as she clambered over the rocks, getting to her feet again, letting her skirt fall, straightening the webbed pistol belt at her right hip, the Detonics Scoremaster there in the military flap holster.

She could see for miles from here. She had started coming here as a little girl and she had never stopped. She didn't remember their home at the farm. Perhaps someday they would go back to where it had stood and something she would see would jog loose a memory—she hoped that it would. But the Retreat was the home she had grown up in, was the home in her heart.

She dropped to her knees, gathering her skirt under her, leaning back, sitting finally, not taking her eyes off the mountains and the valleys between them.

She was cold as the wind picked up and she hugged her arms to her, huddling more in the quilted coat she had made.

She had never known the company of adults of her own sex—and she wondered if she and Paul came together, would they sometime, someday be drawn apart.

She thought of her mother.

The Retreat was not Sarah Rourke's home. It never would be. She hated it—that was obvious, Annie realized.

She thought of her father and her mother—and she was frightened.

She had known nothing else—that Sarah Rourke and John Rourke were husband and wife and that it was forever for them.

Annie Rourke was very cold now. She closed her eyes and saw Paul Rubenstein's face and couldn't imagine feeling toward Paul what her mother now felt toward her father. But then for an instant she could imagine it—and she was afraid.

She was very afraid and she sat there and stared out at the mountains again, wanting Paul Rubenstein to say he loved her, to hold her.

Chapter Forty-Seven

The interior air lock door had not taken as long as the exterior door which had been covered with rock.

"I have it, John," Natalia announced.

Rourke watched her for a moment, then stared at the dismantled locking device. "They never intended their retreat to be unoccupied."

"It was never made to be opened from the outside."

Rourke nodded to her. He looked at his son, Madison standing beside him. "You said this second holy book is some sort of diary."

"It looks like that—one of the videotapes had a diary featured in the story, and I read about diaries."

Rourke nodded. "All right. So we get this second holy book and break the seal and read it."

"That is forbidden—even to ones like yourselves," Madison whispered.

John Rourke put his hands on the girl's shoulders, then smiled at her. "Michael tells me the Bible is very important to the people here—at least to some of you."

"That is true." Madison nodded somberly. "It is

all that we read."

"Then isn't it presumptuous for men—like the ones who head the Families—isn't it presumptuous for men to add to it, to change it, with some secret book they won't even read themselves but that supposedly gives them the authority to commit murder every time the population goes over some magic number, year in, year out, to create people like the ones you call Them, to create people who aren't people anymore at all?"

"But—"

"I look at the story of Adam and Eve rather differently than most people do. If their aim was to seek knowledge, I don't see it as a sin. To play games with the devil—that's wrong. But to want to know, to understand—knowing isn't evil. It's what you do with the knowledge. We'll find that book—you think Natalia's good on doors, wait 'til you see her with a safe. We'll read that book and then we'll know what really happened here and how to help all the Madisons and all the other people here—or at least we'll be better able to try. All right, sweetheart?"

"Yes," and she leaned her head against his chest. "Yes, Father Rourke."

John Rourke just closed his eyes and hugged the girl for a moment.

"We're ready," Natalia said.

Rourke looked at her. "All right."

"I'll go first," Paul announced.

He was already starting to open the doorway, Michael covering him with Rourke's CAR-15.

Then Michael passed through, Rourke hearing him call. "There's no one waiting for us."

"There may be a redoubt of some kind further ahead," Rourke answered.

Madison passed through the doorway then.

Rourke stood alone beside Natalia. She touched at his hand. "If I were a young girl—you would make a fine father."

Rourke looked at her, smiling. "Just because I let myself age another five years while you slept— well, don't rub it in, huh?"

And he let Natalia pass through the doorway and he followed her close behind, a Detonics pistol in each hand.

Chapter Forty-Eight

"The last thing I ever expected to see again in my whole life was a golf course," Paul Rubenstein murmured.

Rourke shrugged—after the indoor pool (Olympic sized) and the sauna and the racquetball courts, an indoor nine-hole golf course hardly surprised him. That it was only nine holes he found curious.

He stepped out onto the perfect green carpet, dropping to one knee—what he felt through the knee of his Levi's, the touch of his fingertips confirmed. Synthetic grass. It had been called

Astroturf before the Night of The War. "I have never seen this place," Madison murmured, between Rourke and his son.

Rourke looked at her. "This place—the Place—it's hermetically sealed at most times—at all times really because of the air lock. No dust, no dirt. No reason for maintenance. The pool is bone dry—likely hasn't been filled for centuries. I bounced one of those racquetballs—the core is dead. It hasn't been used for a long time."

"A playground," Michael murmured.

"The rich capitalist playground." Natalia smiled.

Rourke looked at her. "Yes—isn't it," and he reached up to the Alessi shoulder rig, returning the one Detonics pistol he still held, with his left hand closing the trigger guard snap that formed the speed break. "Let's find that arsenal—then we'll find their book. If they can't use what they have, maybe we can. With that door having to be forced open, the hermetic seal is broken. If those cannibals have an ounce of brains among them they'll feel the air circulating between the crack the door left and the wall—and they'll pry it open and attack. What Michael told us about that one cannibal following him and Madison on a blood hunt—that may be typical behavior. And we killed a lot of them. Now be on the lookout for those guys in the business suits with the cattle prods. Madison—show us the way to the arsenal."

"Yes—where the guns are kept."

"Yes—where the guns are kept." She started

ahead, walking beside and slightly ahead of Michael, her right hand locked inside his left, Michael's right fist balled around the CAR-15's pistol grip, the Colt assault rifle's stock collapsed, the scope covers removed.

Rourke felt a hand touch gently at his—he looked into Natalia's eyes, his left hand closing over her right hand. "He looks so much like you—but he isn't you," and she leaned up quickly as she walked beside him, kissing him on the cheek.

"I love you," John Rourke told her, still holding her hand, walking on.

Chapter Forty-Nine

Natalia had opened the doors to the arsenal—not bothering to pick the lock, instead half wheeling right, a double kick to where the two doors joined, the doors splitting inward.

Paul had rushed in, the subgun ready in case the Families had decided the arsenal should be their redoubt.

But the arsenal was empty of people.

"Who were these people?" Natalia whispered.

Rourke didn't answer her.

"Arsenal—you can say that again," Paul Rubenstein whispered.

Rourke looked at him for an instant, then to the

walls. What he estimated as a hundred M-16s were in racks locked to the wall with retention bars, the bars padlocked. Beyond these, smaller racks, three tiers high, at least fifty Government Model .45s in each of the racks, perhaps a hundred and fifty in all. Beyond these, a solitary glass-fronted rack—Rourke walked toward this and examined what lay beyond the glass. Six Steyr-Mannlicher SSGs, identical to his own rifle which was back at the Retreat.

"My guns!"

Rourke turned around, his son examining the long glass case on the opposite wall. Rourke looked back to the rifle case, his right hand feeling behind it where the case mated to the wall—there was a gap, uneven. "Hmm," he murmured under his breath.

Then he started across the room. The center of the · room—carpeted, which he considered curious—was piled high with wooden and cardboard crates and metal military carry boxes. Ammunition—5.56mm for the M-16s, .45 ACP for the pistols and 7.62mm NATO for the sniper rifles. But there were other boxes as well—commercial ammunition in 9mm Parabellum, .44 Magnum and .357 Magnum, as well as boxes of shotshells, all seemingly twelve gauge, the majority 00 Buck, some rifled slugs as well he noted.

He continued across the room. Natalia stood beside Michael—her attention seeming to shift nervously from the long gun cabinet to the double doors leading back into the corridor.

Rourke looked at the gun cabinet—handguns, an expensive collection, some neatly arranged on fabric-covered pegs, some just lying in the bottom of the cabinet. "Our friends had interesting tastes," Rourke remarked to no one in particular. Smith & Wesson and Colt revolvers, Walther and Browning semi-automatics. Along the bottom of the case mixed in with the handguns, several shotguns—Remington 870s and 1100s, Mossberg 500s of various configurations, Browning Auto Fives. There was a closed leather case which Rourke assumed contained a Browning Superposed and extra barrels.

"This room would have been worth a fortune," Paul Rubenstein said suddenly.

"No," Rourke corrected. "Not this room—at least not originally. This room wasn't the arsenal to begin with—it was some other room. That case holding the sniper rifles—it was removed from its original mountings. And this one," and Rourke bent to the side, feeling along the wall. "This is the same. With the air locks and all, they were security-conscious—you don't leave an arsenal like this in a room a woman can kick her way into without half trying."

"Thank you, not at all." Natalia smiled.

"Even a very special woman. No—there's a vault around here, and if it were important enough to remove this stuff from the vault, then whatever they put in the vault must have been even more important. Stand back," and Rourke waited as Natalia, Michael, Madison and Paul Ruben-

191

stein stepped away from the glass. Rourke stepped back, sidestepped, selecting the spot, then wheeled half right, bending into a double Tae Kwon Do kick into the glass, snapping his foot away, wheeling as the glass shattered, shards of it falling, collapsing.

"What do you do?" Madison asked, her voice alarmed-sounding.

"With those guys outside—we'll need more equipment than we have. This is called liberating."

"John explained it to me once—a long time ago," Paul Rubenstein told her. "Before the Night of The War, taking something just because you needed it was stealing. But since then, taking something you need to stay alive is survival. So it's liberating."

"It's still stealing," Rourke interrupted, "but in a good cause."

Michael already was reaching through the opening broken into the glass—his Stalker, his Predator. Michael checked both guns. "Empty."

"At least they know how to do that." Rourke nodded. Michael slipped the Predator into the trouser band of his Levi's.

"I wonder where the hell they put the rest of my stuff?"

"We'll find it—liberate some ammo for yourself."

Michael reached into the case again, having handed off the Predator to Madison who seemed somehow frightened of holding a gun. Rourke already knew his son well enough—she would get over this fear quickly enough. Guns of themselves were nothing to fear—only some of the people who use them; guns could just as easily be an instrument to eradicate fear.

He watched his son—three Smith & Wesson Model 629s, eight and three-eigths, a six, and a four.

"Don't you think you're overdoing it a little?"

"I like .44s—but you were right, I needed to add something that loads a little faster. These'll do for now."

Rourke only shook his head. "Look in that bin at the far end of the room. See what they have—maybe holsters or whatever." All three of the stainless Smiths were wearing the factory walnut and they wouldn't reload that much faster without speedloaders. He shrugged.

Natalia was taking a Walther P-38 from the cabinet. "One extra pistol will do me nicely. I've used these before. But I'm going to pick the locks on those chains and get us some extra M-16s," and she turned to Madison. "Would you like to help me, darling?"

"All right." Madison followed after her, Michael already by the bins at the far end of the room. "Pachmayr grips, Safariland speedloaders, boxes of spare magazines for all the mazagine-fed weapons."

"Good—take what you think we'll need and get Pachmayrs onto those Smith revolvers. Natalia's got a screwdriver. And take plenty of speed-loaders."

Paul, standing beside Rourke, remarked, "These

people had good taste."

"Take a couple of extra pistols for yourself, Paul—and a couple of M-16s. If we can avoid getting down to stone axes again, I'd just as soon."

"You'd just as soon," Rubenstein laughed.

Rourke watched as the younger man took two blued commercial Browning High Powers, these like the battered military model Rubenstein carried, old enough to have the cone hammers rather than the spur type hammers similar to those on the Colt Government Model.

Rubenstein started toward the bins, Rourke still standing before the shattered case. They would return what they had taken if the situation warranted it—as much as he joked about it, liberating was still a form of stealing, even when necessary. But he knew what he would "borrow" at least. He had given his to Annie. And there were two here—Detonics Scoremaster .45s, the cone hammered, flat mainspring housing stainless steel Detonics counterpart to the Colt Gold Cup.

He took the two pistols into his hands—they were factory original except that the once sharp corners of the high profile Bo-Mar rear sights had been rounded off. As he closed his fists over the Pachmayr gripped butts, the beavertail grip safeties deactivated.

There was a good feel to the guns. He would regret having to return them, but he would.

He started toward the bins, to find spare magazines if there were any.

Chapter Fifty

John Rourke stood in the doorway between the arsenal room and the corridor, Natalia watching him. The two stainless steel Scoremasters were positioned, each butt rightward in his trouser band and under his pistol belt—she had watched as he'd tested then loaded the dozen or so spare magazines he had found, then stuffed them into his musette bag. He carried an M-16 now in addition to his CAR-15.

She looked at Michael—John's near-identical duplicate. He had found his own M-16, the one he had taken from the Retreat, a second one carried on his left side now. She had taken a second M-16 for herself as well. Michael's liberated Smith & Wesson pistols he now carried—all three of them, in two wide cartridge looped belts, the belts crisscrossing at his hips, holsters for them to match. Safariland, like her own.

Madison carried two M-16s, but the girl carried them only to carry them, knowing nothing of guns yet, looking incongruous in the gray maid's uniform and small white apron with an assault rifle under each arm. She was a pretty girl—but she was seemingly bewildered by the newness of her relationship with Michael, bewildered by Michael's father, and his father's friends, and by the terror she had seen. Natalia blamed the girl not at all for the latter, and the other sources of the girl's bewilderment would pass with time. They had passed for her, Natalia remembered.

Paul had found a double holster rig for the two Browning High Powers and wore this now, having added an M-16. But the assault rifle slung across his back, the Schmeisser, as he called the MP-40, he grasped in his hands.

Natalia started toward the doorway now, her liberated P-38 in what she recognized as a German police full flap holster added to her belt with the L-Frame Smiths.

She had taken one other thing from the arsenal—a Randall Model 12 Smithsonian Bowie. The blade was eleven inches long, two and one quarter inches deep, the stock three-eighths inches thick. She had seen them before the Night of The War and with her penchant for knives had always wanted one. At least this was hers to borrow. Made for a large man, weighing she judged a good two pounds, the leather washed handle was large enough that she could hold it with two hands comfortably and thus wield it like a short sword. This hung in its scabbard behind the butt of the L-Frame on her left side.

She stopped at the doorway. "Now what, John?"

Rourke nodded. "Paul—you take Madison and her M-16s there and go back near the doors where we hid the bikes. Any sign of the guys from outside, open fire and we'll be there—we should hear gunfire well enough anywhere in the complex. It doesn't seem they were too concerned with deadening sound when they built this place. Natalia and Michael and I'll go through the complex—find that book Michael talked about and look for the vault these gun cases were removed from. Between the book and the vault, we should have our answers."

"All right—you guys be careful, huh?"

Rourke clapped his friend on the shoulder. "Aren't we always?"

"Yeah, well, if there weren't two ladies present I'd tell ya about that." Natalia watched Paul turn to look at Madison. "You ready, Madison?"

"Yes—" but she looked past Paul at Michael. "Be careful, please."

Michael leaned past Paul and kissed her quickly on the lips. Paul took her hand and started back along the corridor with her.

"Which way do we go now?" Natalia asked, looking at Michael.

"Just to the end of the corridor—double doors, like a conference room. It's where the Ministers talked to me. Where they had the wall safe with the second holy book," and he looked at his father. "What about this room—you always taught me never to leave any guns behind."

Natalia smiled. "Paul and I took care of that— the M-16s don't have any firing pins, neither do the semi-automatic pistols. The shotguns and the revolvers we didn't have time for."

"It'll have to do," John Rourke announced. "So—let's find that second holy book."

John Rourke started into the corridor, Natalia beside him, Michael—as she looked back—coming behind.

Chapter Fifty-One

She had picked the lock in less than a minute and John Rourke—wearing his heavy leather gloves—had opened the doors, remembering Michael's experience with the electrified door handles. So far, there had been no sign of anyone from the Families or from the servants. No one.

Rourke walked through the doorway into the conference room.

"There—over there's the safe, behind that," and Michael stared toward it.

"Wait, Michael—it may be electrified," Natalia called after him.

Rourke joined them, eyeing the doorway, still wearing his gloves, gingerly touching at the wood carving and exposing the safe.

Rourke drew the Gerber knife from his left hip and touched the tip to the safe door, to the combination lock, to the handle—there was no sparking as there would be if it were electrified.

"Go to work," Rourke told her.

"I don't have my stethoscope."

"I have mine on my bike."

"But I won't need it for a little wall safe," she finished.

Rourke nodded, turning away from the safe to study the murals—the Night of The War, the holocaust when the sky took flame, although he imagined the latter was largely based on supposition and the terrified tales of any who had been caught outside and made it inside as the sky had caught fire.

The candles on the table near the largest of the two large chairs. He approached these, removing his right glove, touching at the wax at the top—it was still warm. "They didn't leave here too long ago," he announced. He felt the chair—the seat was still warm. "Hmm," he murmured.

He looked at the walls again—at the massive wooden carving on the rear wall. "Hmm."

"I have it," Natalia called.

Rourke turned back to look at her standing beside the wall safe. In her right hand she held the small book which Rourke assumed to be the one of which Michael had spoken.

"That's it," Michael confirmed, as if reading Rourke's thoughts. Rourke smiled at the possibility.

"It's a diary. I used a cover identity for six months once as an American housewife—I used one of these as a prop. These locks can be opened with a bobby pin."

"Do you have a bobby pin?" Rourke asked her, smiling, standing beside her now.

"I may in my purse."

"Never mind," he interrupted. He withdrew the Gerber from its sheath. "These things can be opened this way, too."

He pried gently with the Gerber's tip where the two portions of the lock met.

"Have you opened many diaries, John?"

He laughed. "Don't forget—espionage was my

racket too for a few years," and the lock popped.

He handed the book to Michael. "Your discovery. Read it—unless you don't want to."

Michael took the diary, saying nothing, then opening it.

Rourke walked over to the nearest of the chairs at the conference table, drawing the two stainless Detonics Scoremaster .45s from where they were nestled against his abdomen, placing them on the conference table beside him.

Michael began to read. "We have committed an unspeakable crime against God and against humanity."

Michael looked up from the diary. John Rourke thought that instant that secrets were rarely kept secrets to hide their beauty.

Chapter Fifty-Two

Michael continued to read. "I have set forth here an account of our actions taken in order to survive after the horror of the burning in the sky. It is a brief account because I cannot bring myself to dwell on the details lest I should weep—"

"A rather quaint style, isn't it?" John Rourke observed.

"I'm skipping some more of his recriminations —here—here—" and Michael began again to read from the diary. "When the flames seared the sky, it was evident to all of us that in order to live, the survival retreat erected by our employers—"

"Their employers," Natalia whispered.

"Let him go on," Rourke told her. He took a cigar from inside his battered brown bomber jacket and lit it in the flame of his Zippo—there was no ash tray but the fact didn't bother him.

"The survival retreat erected by our employers would have to be hermetically sealed by means of the air locks for some time. Food supplies immediately began to dwindle despite the best rationing methods instituted by our employers and augmented by the kitchen staff. After several weeks, a volunteer from among the servants was sent out through the air locks to see if the atmosphere was safe. He was never heard from again. There was an attitude among us, those who served, that life had ceased having meaning. Although we were brought to our employers' survival retreat prior to the bombings and missile strikes, our families and loved ones and friends were not. There were a few fortunates among us whose entire immediate family was in service, and therefore not excluded from the survival retreat. After several weeks, the rationing now quite severe, the air quality poor, another volunteer set forth. Likewise, he was never heard from again. It seemed clear that two choices confronted the persons living in the survival retreat, masters and servants alike—to either die a slow death or commit suicide. But it was one of the employers who struck on a third alternative, though it was never ascertained which of them, for indeed he may well have been killed in the fighting—"

"Oh, my God," Natalia murmured.

Michael looked up a moment, then back to his diary. "The employers decided to exile their servants to whatever lay beyond the hermetically sealed doors. It was, as discussion amongst us later brought forth, only a logical extension of their view of us, their servants. For, after all, did we not exist to fulfill their needs? This then—survival—was a need like any other.

"They awakened us while we slept, most of us in our pajamas or nightgowns forced from the quarters below and assembled at gunpoint on the golf course. We were then herded like animals into a pen in the swimming pool which had never been filled. We were held there, as two at a time our numbers depleted. But those taken away never returned. And suddenly, the whispered fate of these our co-workers began to spread throughout those of us who remained. Our co-workers, in some cases members of our families—they had been sent to their deaths through the air lock doors. One of our number—a brave soul—shouted this to our employers, that we, the servants, were being systematically executed. The employer—a boy of fourteen—nearest him shot him in the face with one of the rifles taken from storage in the arsenal vault. A cry went up. One of the butlers clambered up the side of the swimming pool to disarm the young murderer. One of the employers shot him, then smashed in his skull with the butt of a rifle. One of the parlor maids screamed, running toward the ladder leading from the pool. She was kicked back. More of our numbers then— it had begun. We started from the pool, many of us dying before ever reaching the level of those who would systematically murder us. There was fighting, shouting and much killing on both sides. I myself picked up a rifle and killed my employer with it, and then in a fit of rage shot his oldest son, shot his wife, shot his youngest daughter. His oldest daughter fell to her knees at my feet and wept. I did not shoot her. After the employers had been subdued, it was decided that indeed their decision to reduce the population of the survival retreat had been the only valid choice for survival. So the population was reduced. The bodies pushed through the air lock were some of the employers. The surviving employers were locked in their quarters and guarded. That night, I made love to my employer's eldest daughter whose life I had spared and throughout it, I felt that she laughed inside herself at me."

Michael looked up from the diary. "I can't read any more of this."

Natalia—abruptly—took the diary from Michael's hands. She continued after a moment— Rourke presumed spent locating Michael's place —to read. "Several weeks passed and we soon realized that the employers had needed us. We had not needed them. But still, there were very few of us. Selected younger members of the employers'

203

families—the woman whose bed I shared among them—were taken under tutelage and shown how best to prepare meals, to tend the gardens which grew beneath the artificial light, to clean what needed to be cleaned about the survival retreat of which we now were the masters. The chief butler among us was skilled with mathematical computations and with the cooperation and intelligence of the chief gardener, the food supply's yield was calculated. Twenty-four of the new masters—among these myself—had survived. More than one hundred of the former masters, the employers, remained. But by best estimates, only one hundred people could be supported by the garden without overtaxing the soil, without overusing the grow lights. Realizing that only one hundred could survive, those of us who now held sway drew random lots from among the more than one hundred of our employers. Twenty-nine names were selected, among these the oldest and least fit to work, to survive. In the dark of night when the lights were turned off, by candlelight we moved through the corridors—at gunpoint, we forced these selected ones toward the air lock doors. And then we turned them out to die."

Natalia looked up, almost whispering, "I wish I had cigarettes."

Rourke watched her eyes as they flickered back to the diary. "The population began by natural means to grow and there was little illness. Again, from among the employers there were names selected. The employer's daughter whom I had

204

made my wife had borne me a child and though her name was selected, my wife's name was set aside and another was chosen. As the years passed and it was realized that the earth outside our home beneath the ground might never be restored to where it could support life, those of the original group of servants who survived as the new masters formed the Counsel of Ministers in order to assume the awesome responsibility of determining who would live and who would go through the doors to their death, this to spare the greatest numbers any guilt. Voluntarily, our segment of the population was limited to twenty-four, meaning that seventy-six of our former employers, now our servants, would be permitted. When a child was born to us, the new masters, our population would be one or perhaps two too great. When a child was born to the new servants, their population would be too high as well. It was at these times that the Counsel of Ministers—Ministers because we prayed for guidance in our choices and prayed for the remission of our continual sins—we would determine from among the new servants who would die. It could not be done by lot—the gardeners were important, too important often to die. The lower classes of servants were used—the tailors, the seamstresses. Fibrous plants were grown and their bounty converted to cloth from which clothing could be fashioned with great skill. Slippers were worn because there was no leather for shoes. Life continued among both classes while inexorably, birth would come and death would be selected. No longer could only the old or infirm be selected to go, but from among the young.

"I write this as I lay in the bed of my death—and I welcome death as death has come to be welcomed by all of our class, for death saves another life from being taken. And this is my consolation, that when my death comes, there will be ninety-nine only among all who dwell here and when a new child is born, no one will need to go. May God forgive me and all like me for what I was forced to do."

Natalia closed the book.

John Rourke looked at his son. "They don't know of this—the Ministers? They don't know what is contained in the diary?"

"I think the old one does—he carries a key. It's his badge of office. He told me he didn't know—"

Natalia interrupted. "If this diary has been locked for nearly five centuries, and John opened it by prying the lock with his knife, then why are there fresh scratches near the keyhole?"

Rourke looked at her.

Michael whispered, "He did read it—the old one read it."

John Rourke closed his eyes. He spoke. "The old one you talked of—he revered the diary too much to destroy it. You told him of the aircraft and the pilot. You told him about us—the Retreat. All his life, he thought he'd been carrying out some preordained mission of murder based on some holy book. Now he finds it's the diary of a murderer and that all he's been doing is carrying

206

out a tradition of killing the innocent."

"His mind might—"

Rourke looked at his son. "That weapons vault is the only place they could be—all the people from here. I think I know what we'll find once we locate it." And John Rourke felt Natalia hold his right arm very tightly as he picked up the twin stainless Scoremasters from the conference table.

Chapter Fifty-Three

Paul Rubenstein stayed near the inside of the air lock, listening—but there was no sound from outside. Behind him, he heard Madison speak. "The woman with Michael's father—she cannot be his mother. She is too young. Michael's father seems too young—he looks almost not at all older than Michael."

Paul looked at her and smiled. "That's a long story. Michael's mother is at our place—our Retreat. And Natalia is John Rourke's friend."

"But Michael's father and the woman Natalia—they look at each other like Michael looks at me, like I look at Michael."

Rubenstein shrugged. "I told you—it's a long story. But you're right—I know the look. There's a girl—Michael's sister. Her name is Annie. You'll like her, Madison—and she looks at me that way," and he smiled inside himself, feeling the smile as it crossed his lips. "That probably sounds real peculiar. Well, but—"

"I think that you are a good man. That is what she smiles at."

Paul Rubenstein studied her face a moment. Then he replied, "Thank you—very much," and he looked away rather than feel more embarrassed than he already felt. That no one came through the doors as yet somehow frightened him more than if dozens of the cannibals were attacking. And what had become of the people who lived here?

He shivered, shaking his shoulders, flexing the muscles there to shake off the feeling.

The Schmeisser in his hands, he crouched beside the door. "Madison—remember, keep a lookout behind us."

"I remember," the girl answered.

Flexing his shoulder muscles had not gotten rid of the feeling.

Chapter Fifty-Four

John Rourke spoke as he ran, Natalia and Michael flanking him as they turned from one corridor into the next. "Think about it. Once they realized the ones they called Them were outside, when the Ministers and the rest of the uppercrust died, they wouldn't consign their bodies to be eaten. Assuming that the air was at least marginally breathable at least a century ago, that accounts for moving the arms from the vault. They're using the original vault which would have been sealable as a burial chamber for the Families. If your husband or wife or child died, could you send their body through the air lock to be ripped to pieces?"

"But where is it?" Natalia asked, panting. Rourke's own body, he realized, was tiring more rapidly because of the prolonged exposure to the thinner air—Natalia's as well. But Michael, who had lived in the thinner atmosphere for fifteen years, in this heavier atmosphere inside the Place, more like the atmosphere that had once been upon the surface of the earth, seemed to thrive. They stopped at the mouth of a corridor they had not yet explored.

Rourke stared along its length—a massive gray steel door at the far end.

"The vault," Natalia whispered.

Michael started—very slowly—walking around it, saying, "If they knew we had found our way inside and that the air lock's integrity was broken and that the cannibals would—" He let the sentence hang.

"A fear built for a century," Natalia whispered.

"They'd look at it as a final decent act—the old one and the other Ministers," Rourke added. Rourke held the liberated M-16's pistol grip in his right fist. He looked at his son. "When the cannibals had Madison before you tried to get her out, were they about to—"

"No," Michael answered quickly.

"Did Madison say why she wasn't a breeder?"

"No, she—what the hell are you—"

"I don't know yet—I'm thinking out loud. Forget about it," and John Rourke walked ahead. If it were nothing with Madison—he suddenly remembered during the fighting. He had given one of the cannibals a knee smash and it had had virtually no effect.

He stopped at the vault door. His gloves were on but he wouldn't risk it—he took the black chrome A.G. Russell Sting IA from inside his trouser band, gently tossing the knife toward the door. There was no sparking of electricity.

He picked up the knife, re-sheathing it.

He touched the flash deflectored muzzle of the M-16 to the combination dial, then to the opening handle of the vault door, holding the M-16 by the synthetic buttstock only. There was no sparking of electricity either time.

He looked to his right—double doors, the kind that swung inward and outward, but a chain looped through the door handles and drawn tight, a padlock on the chain.

"Natalia—work on cracking the vault. Michael—keep her covered. Call me when it's open."

"Where are you going?" his son called from behind him. "What are—"

"Do as I said," Rourke answered softly.

Rourke stopped a good fifty feet from the

chained double doors. He shouldered the M-16, the selector set to semi. He sighted on the chain link rather than the lock, firing.

"What are you—"

"Never mind!" It had been a miss. He fired again, connecting, but the chain didn't break.

"You want the chain broken—just tell me about it," Michael called from behind him.

Rourke lowered his rifle, then nodded. "I'm sorry I lost my temper. So use your cannon and break the chain."

Michael stood beside him now, the Magnum Sales Stalker extended in both fists before him.

"Hold your ears, Natalia," Rourke called, covering his own ears. The gleaming stainless steel revolver bucked once in Michael's hands and he lowered it a moment, then raised it again to sight through the scope. The revolver fired again. Michael turned to his father. Rourke took his hands from his ears. "You watch yourself with that thing shooting indoors—gonna mess up your hearing."

"What?" and Michael laughed. "I couldn't hear you."

Rourke feigned a punch toward his son's midsection, Michael dodging, laughing. Rourke felt two things inside himself as he walked toward the double doors, the lock shattered and obviously so—gladness for having Michael, and a sickness for what he thought he would find beyond the doors.

Chapter Fifty-Five

Rourke stood in the center of the room. Michael had gone back to Natalia.

There was a single stainless steel surgical table. Beside it was a covered tray. He lifted the covering from the tray, folding back the white cloth.

He closed his eyes.

The Ministers had many sins.

He opened his eyes.

He turned away and left the room, but something caught his eye as he did and he stopped. Rourke walked toward a nearly emptied surgical cabinet. The top shelf held a large mortar and pestle.

The middle shelf was empty as was the lower shelf.

There was fine dust in the bowl of the pestle— Madison had spoken of never experiencing medical treatment. Michael had said the old one seemed to consider it a sin to attempt to prolong life. It was possible that the Ministers cheated on this, but Rourke doubted it.

Then there was only one other answer.

He shook his head and walked from the room.

He could see Natalia—she was on her knees by the combination dial for the vault.

Rourke kept walking, feeling very tired. He stopped, beside Natalia, handing Michael his M-16. "Stand up—and hold me—please," and he watched her eyes as she looked up at him, as she got from her knees, as she looked at him again, then her arms folding around him and Rourke leaned his face against her head. His voice sounded off to him. "I thought we were through with it, ya know? With all this insanity. Karamatsov is gone. Rozhdestvenskiy is gone. I thought it was all gone with them. I really did. And then these cannibals—" Rourke felt Natalia's hands touch at his neck—their coolness, their softness. "I really thought that after all of this—" and he laughed, holding her body tight against him. He felt Michael's hand on his shoulder. "I really—"

"Dad, what—"

Rourke licked his lips. He looked up, at his son, and at the woman he had not been supposed to love but did. "Inside that room—it's a very basic surgery. I found tools—the kind you'd only use for one thing. And then evidence they were making pills—and two empty shelves. We're going to open that vault—and every single person from here—"

"I found the combination. All I have to do is—"

"I'll do it. Don't come in unless I tell you to."

"I can—"

"Please," Rourke whispered, and he stepped away from Natalia a single step. He leaned his lips to her forehead, touching her there. Then he turned to the vault door. He placed his left hand on the handle.

"You want your rifle, Dad?" Michael asked.

Rourke only shook his head. He worked the handle downward hard, then pulled on the vault door, swinging it open. "Don't go inside," he whispered, going inside.

The overhead light bulbs—he imagined they had found a way of making their own filaments and reusing the bulbs—were bright. He could see clearly.

Nearly one hundred people—seven men in three-piece business suits and red bedroom slippers; seven women in elaborate re-creations of high fashion dresses from five centuries ago (but they too, incongruously, wore the red slippers); a half dozen children, two boys and four girls, in fashionably expensive looking clothing from five centuries ago, wearing diminutive versions of the red slippers; roughly seventy-five men and women and children in gray slippers, the men wearing the off-white jackets of busboys, the women in severe gray maids' uniforms, the children dressed identically to the older members of their caste. Infants as well. A few of the business-suited men were missing—the ones from the fight in the cave and the attack of the cannibals, Rourke surmised. Those men were dead. And so was everyone in the room.

Rourke dropped to his knees beside the body of a dead little boy—one of the servant class, a descendant of one of the former masters who had begun it all five centuries earlier. Rourke's right hand reached out to the boy, the boy sitting against the back of a man, a woman's head resting in the boy's lap. Rourke closed the boy's eyes, and then he closed his own. . . .

"Dad!"

Rourke didn't open his eyes. "Stay outside with Natalia, son," and then he opened his eyes and he stood, staring down at the dead clustered around him.

He began to walk the length of the vault, stepping over the dead, stopping to examine a dead child or a dead woman or a dead man to be certain—but they were all dead.

He found the old one, knowing it was the man Michael had spoken of. The watch chain—Rourke held up the key, letting it sway a moment pendulum fashion.

Rourke shook his head, then bent to the man—he replaced the key and closed the man's eyes.

The far end of the room—he started toward it now. Cloth bags were there—the shapes were enough to show him, stacked one atop the other. Generations of the Families.

He looked at the old one. "For what?" John Rourke whispered.

He would not have expected an answer even if any of them had remained alive.

There was a dead woman near his feet as he stopped near the vault door, her eyes dull but once pretty he knew. He looked at her right hand as he closed her eyes—the skin was rough textured from toil. If it were a symbol of poetic justice for the sins of her ancestors—if all of it were that, John Rourke thought. He shook his head, "Aww, shit," and he stood up and walked back to the living.

Chapter Fifty-Six

"They're all dead—mass murder or mass suicide, I don't know which," Rourke told them as he walked, again Natalia and Michael flanking him. "The surgery was used for castrations—the Counsel of Ministers realized what they had done sending people out into the outside world. Some of them survived by eating the others and there was no other way for the Ministers to reduce their population without sending out surplus people. So, they castrated the men. The reason we only saw men outside was because of the few who were strong enough to stay alive and be accepted into the cannibals—the ones Madison calls Them—none were women." And he looked at Natalia. "Even if you were out there, with no weapons, no martial arts training—you wouldn't have had a prayer."

"I disagree," Natalia said flatly.

Rourke put his right arm around her shoulders for an instant, then found her left hand and held it as they continued walking. "Likely the cannibals had enough sense left that when their numbers began dwindling, they'd let new members in—and the food was less needed. Population control for the outside world as well. Involuntary—just like it was inside. You said," and he looked at Michael, "that one or two of them shouted 'meat' as they attacked. They were probably some of the more recent acquisitions to the tribe—they still retained some language that was recognizable. There isn't any village—they wander, eating what they can off the land and waiting for their ration of meat. And they were never disappointed. Never at all. But they can't reproduce sexually at all. And with their meat supply gone, some of them will starve to death and the rest of them will just die off naturally. Ten years from now, maybe twenty—none of them will be left. It'll be as if none of them ever existed. A five-centuries-old tribe, which split in two, completely extinct—except for Madison. Some of them—some of them out there now. Some of them still probably have language abilities, but using language like we know it would have been so rare that it just ceased being necessary. Some of them—we could probably talk with them, bring the language back to them."

"Isn't there anything we can do?" Michael asked.

"For Them—nothing. Their religion, their lifestyle, their ritual—all of it tied to receiving the human sacrifices. And they won't have that anymore. We could try to teach them other ways—but they wouldn't let us." He had locked the vault door and taken Michael's revolver and from a safe distance shot off the combination dial. It could never be opened without torches or explosives. "We have to get all the useful stuff from here that we can carry, then make it away from here."

"Madison told me there were rumored to be other exits from here."

"I could look for them—if we could find

217

another way out, we could avoid another battle with the people outside. I don't—"

Rourke looked at Natalia. "Agreed—there's been enough death. Meet us back at the arsenal room—and be careful."

Natalia started to turn off and Rourke reached out to her. She looked back at him. "One hour or less," and she glanced to the gold ladies' Rolex on her left wrist, her left hand held in his right.

"Agreed—one hour."

Rourke watched after her a moment and then tapped his son on the shoulder. "You're a strong young man—that means you can carry a lot of stuff to the bikes. Come on."

Rourke started toward the arsenal room, his son beside him.

Chapter Fifty-Seven

She felt bone weary—the travel and the exertion through the thinner air had sapped her strength, she knew. But she forced herself into the gentle run as she moved along the corridor toward the conference room, one of the M-16s held at high port in her balled fists.

She stopped, before the conference room doors.

She started through, inside, past the conference table and the still-open safe, slowing now, stopping before the rear wall of the conference room. She had seen executive quarters in all parts of the world—the Kremlin, Washington, the corporation boardrooms of New York, Zurich. There was always a secret way in and out.

"Always," she whispered.

As she began examining the wall surfaces, she thought of John Rourke—of his sadness. He had wanted for the world to be changed, for the evil to be gone from it. He had always, she knew, considered her naive. She smiled at the thought—for once she was the realist.

Evil was as intrinsic to life as good.

Her left hand stopped—she found a seam. Her right hand had the Bali-Song, the knife flicking open in her hand, the tip of the Wee-Hawk blade following the seam now, scratching the paint ever so slightly, but giving the seam in the wall greater definition.

She dropped to a crouch, wiping the blade clean on the carpet, flicking the handle half to close the knife, thumbing closed the lock as she squeezed the handles tight together. She pocketed the Bali-Song, feeling down the length of the wall to the floor, a smile something she could feel on her lips as she found the floor seam, following this as well—she had found the door.

She followed the seam out to where it stopped.

Natalia Anastasia Tiemerovna had one task remaining as she glanced at her ladies' Rolex— more than a half hour remained before the rendezvous with John and Michael. She only had to find a way to open the secret door.

Chapter Fifty-Eight

With Michael, Rourke had emptied the arsenal room of all that the bikes could conceivably carry. He had taken no more M-16s—there was an abundance of the rifles and the ammo for them already stored at the Retreat, nor had he taken .45s, and for the same reason. The six Steyr-Mannlicher SSGs were the only long guns he considered potentially useful from the arsenal, spare magazines for these as well and several canisters of .308 to feed the sniper rifles. .44 Magnum ammo for Michael and 9mm Parabellum for Paul Rubenstein and for the Walther P-38 pistol Natalia had selected. A half dozen boxes of .380 ACP for Natalia's stainless PPK/S American, the silenced pistol she had carried in the final assault against the Womb. A stainless steel six-inch Python from the pistol cabinet, then considering, a second one, as well. Perhaps for Annie, perhaps just to hold in reserve.

He had sent Michael on alone with the last batch of weapons and ammo for them, working feverishly to deactivate the weapons Natalia and Paul had not had the time to take care of earlier. To reactivate them, a machinist with gunsmithing abilities would be needed—he doubted any of the cannibals would qualify.

He replaced the last of the revolvers—the firing pin removed—in the cabinet, dropping the firing pin with the others in the musette bag at his left side. He turned when he heard the sound of fingers rapping against a door frame, one of the Detonics Scoremasters coming from his trouser band into his right fist.

But it was Natalia.

She was smiling. "I found our door. Another air lock. It looks as though it was never used. I opened it. It leads out on the far side of the mountain—there's a valley beyond, I climbed up some distance. I got our bearings. We can ride through the valley and then go directly south for perhaps a day and then turn east and intersect our original trail here. It should even save us a day's travel time and the path down from the doorway isn't so steep that we can't walk the bikes."

"What can I say?" Rourke smiled.

"I know what you'll say. Go get Michael and Paul and Madison and meet you by the doorway."

"Where is it?"

"In the back wall of the conference room."

Rourke started toward the doorway. "We'll get the others together—come on," and he took her hand in his and started into the corridor.

Chapter Fifty-Nine

"Madison showed me the hydroelectric power plant for this place—it was only a matter of time. No one had repaired or serviced the generators for so long some of the parts were starting to seize with rust. They would have lost their electrical power here in another year at the most. And the backup generator was so heavily greased it wouldn't have functioned," Michael announced, walking beside his father.

Rourke only nodded, turning into the corridor which led toward the conference room. He glanced back once—Michael was wheeling one of the Harleys, Paul another and Natalia a third. Madison—like Rourke—was festooned with armament, bringing up the rear.

"When we reach those doors, Natalia, you go first to lead the way—I'll leave last in case anything goes wrong inside here," Rourke ordered. They were at the conference room doors now and Rourke stopped, letting Michael roll the Low Rider past him, then letting Natalia and Paul do the same with the other two bikes.

As Madison passed through, looking nervously behind her, Rourke fell into step with her. "Relax," he told her. "The worst is over—you and Michael will be happy together."

"But this place—the Place—I—"

"It's all right now—don't worry, you're safe," and he stopped near the head of the conference table, Natalia pulling open the inside air lock door, Paul Rubenstein helping her.

Natalia looked back once. "It's very steep seeming—but it can be walked without difficulty, you'll find. We'll each need help getting the bikes over the door flanges here and beyond."

"Natalia can help me after I help her, John," the younger man volunteered.

"I'll take care of it on this end—Natalia, be careful," Rourke told her matter-of-factly.

Natalia smiled, nodding. Rourke stepped to the other side of her bike, helping her roll the Harley over the inside air lock flange—the air lock was similar to the type found on a submarine and, Rourke theorized, likely bought from surplus or manufactured to naval specifications in the same factory.

Natalia's bike was through, Rourke helping Rubenstein then. He heard Paul Rubenstein's voice from beyond the interior air lock door. "Wait up a minute—have Michael wait—crowded in here—too crowded."

"Right," Rourke called back—he looked at his son, standing beside Madison. "You two are next," he told them. And then Rourke heard another sound—almost too low to hear but his hearing had always been good and he had always trained himself to listen for sounds that shouldn't be there.

This was such a sound—almost impossible to discern, it was the guttural cry of one of the cannibals and it came from beyond the conference room doors and somewhere inside the Place.

Chapter Sixty

Michael had pushed Madison through the inside air lock door and swung his M-16 forward so rapidly that momentarily Rourke had been shocked by his son's instant apprehension of the danger. He was learning, John Rourke thought.

Rourke started toward the conference room doors, running now, the M-16 in his right hand. He called to his son, his voice a rasping whisper, "Don't open fire—don't make any loud noises. Let's keep 'em searching for us long enough to get everyone through. You go back—get Madison on the back of one of the bikes and ride like hell."

"I'm staying with you. We're—"

"Fighting together, that's just what we're doing. But the more people we have to get through that air lock the longer it'll take. Just do as I say— I'm not plannin' to wait around any longer than I have to. Have Paul ride with you—Natalia can be the last away. She's gonna have to wait for me— we're sharing the same bike."

His son's brown eyes could only be described by one word, Rourke thought—intense. Michael Rourke extended his right hand. "Dad—"

Rourke took his son's hand in his, then folded

his arms around him. "I love you—now get out of here."

He felt the pressure of his son's arms embrace him for a moment, then Michael was starting in a long-strided run back toward the air lock. "If you aren't following us in five minutes—well, Paul can carry double on his bike too and I'll be back, Dad."

Rourke smiled at his son. "I know you will—now hurry," and Michael started the last bike through the interior air lock door.

Rourke worked the selector of the M-16 to auto, waiting. Rolling back the knit cuff of his battered brown bomber jacket, he glanced at the luminous black face of the Rolex Submariner—he would give Michael and the others three minutes only. No more would be needed.

Rourke reached into his inside jacket pocket—he clamped the cigar, unlit, between his teeth, biting down hard on it, waiting. The shouts, the cries—they grew louder now.

Footsteps behind him—Rourke wheeled, the M-16 low, his finger nearly touching the trigger. "Natalia—what the hell are—"

"Paul and I decided. Michael and Madison can make it on their own—Paul's outside with the bikes."

Rourke shook his head, then turned back to the doorway, Natalia taking the opposite side, an M-16 locked in each fist. "When they come," Rourke told her, "empty your guns down the center of the corridor and run for it. I'll be right behind you."

"Agreed—I love you."

"I love you too—what the hell we're gonna do about it, I don't know."

"Sarah will change her mind."

"I don't think so—but she's still my wife."

"I understand that—I always have. It doesn't change how I feel."

"I know that," Rourke told her. "I'm sorry—"

"For the way you are? Don't be—don't ever be, John. If someday—well, then we will. But I don't need that to love you, do you know that?"

"Yes," Rourke almost whispered. "I'm glad you're with me."

He saw them—the first of the cannibals as they raced along the corridor from where the corridor bent. "Don't shoot yet," Rourke commanded. "I want the whole corridor full of them."

Natalia didn't answer. Rourke shifted the M-16 from his right fist into his left. With his right hand, he drew one of the recently liberated Detonics Scoremaster pistols, jacking back the hammer, the chamber already loaded in this pistol as well as its twin still tucked into his belt.

More of the cannibals, the cannibals filling the corridor. "Now!" Rourke shouted, pumping the M-16's trigger in a three-round burst, Natalia stepping into the doorway, both M-16s spitting fire from her hands, the Scoremaster in Rourke's right fist bucking again and again, waves of the cannibals going down, stone clubs launched toward them, falling just short of the doorway.

"Empty!" Natalia shouted.

"Run for it—I'll cover you!"

Rourke's M-16 empty as well, two shots remained in the Scoremaster—Rourke fired them off, ramming the gun, slide locked open, into his waistband, drawing the second Scoremaster with his left fist, firing into the attacking cannibals. He started backing away from the doorway, more of them coming, many of them already wounded and bleeding. The second Scoremaster was empty. Slide locked open, he rammed this into his belt as well.

The twin Detonics stainless Combat Masters— both fists found them, ripping them from the double Alessi shoulder rig, his thumbs jacking back the hammers.

He was at the air lock doorway, cannibals charging now through the conference room doorway, Rourke's index fingers twitching against the triggers, bodies going down.

One pistol empty—the second empty now. Rourke turned, stepping through the doorway, throwing his weight against the air lock door, feeling suddenly weight—pushing at it. Then more weight as he threw his body against it—the door was being pushed open against him.

A hand through the space between the door and the frame. The A.G. Russel Sting IA—Rourke stabbed the back of the hand with the small bladed knife, a scream of pain, a spurt of blood, the hand drawn back. Rourke dropped the knife.

Behind him—Natalia's voice. "John, run for it—we can get the second door together."

Rourke reached down for the Sting IA and ran, diving through the second door, rolling onto the rocks beyond, twisting, clambering to his feet, throwing his weight against the exterior air lock door, Natalia beside him. But the door would not close. "Paul!"

But Rubenstein was already beside them. "Who the hell's on the other side of that door?"

"A bunch of determined guys who don't know any better—rugged outdoor life they lead, all that crap. Now push," Rourke snarled, leaning into it as he fought the door.

"It's no good!" Natalia shouted.

Rourke glanced behind him once, chewing down harder on his cigar. "Natalia, start Paul's bike—then start our bike. Paul—when I count to five, make a run for your bike and—"

"It's too steep that way," Natalia interrupted. "We'll have to cut across the mountain—there's a better path on the far side that we can ride down."

"You heard her—then cut across. Natalia and I'll be right behind you."

"I'll lay down some fire once you guys get rollin'."

"Right." Rourke nodded to the younger man. "Natalia—get the bikes started."

Natalia moved away from the air lock door, Rourke throwing his weight hard against it now—it was the first time he had realized how strong Natalia was, despite her size.

The roar of one of the Harley's coming to life. The sound of an engine being gunned again and again.

More pressure against the door.

The sound of the second Harley starting, Rourke shouting to Paul Rubenstein. "Run for it—go on!"

"Count of five?"

"One—two—three—four—FIVE!"

"See ya," and Paul Rubenstein jumped back from the door, running, Rourke looking back once as the younger man mounted his machine, the engine revving once, then the bike tearing off across the mountain top.

"I'm ready," Natalia shouted.

Rourke looked back at her—both M-16s were leveled at the doorway.

"Now!" Rourke released the door, half stumbling back, hitting the rock surface, the door flying open, cannibals starting to pour from inside, Natalia's M-16s firing over his head, Rourke dragging himself across the rock surface, clear of her guns now, to his feet.

He straddled the Jet Black Low Rider, shouting to Natalia as he rammed fresh magazines into the little Detonics pistols, then stuffed them back in his side pockets. "Now!"

The gunfire ceased, shouts and the bizarre speech of the cannibals filling the air—the pressure of Natalia on the bike, her hands tapping his shoulders, the pressure of her arms around his waist as he gunned the bike, away, the blur of a stone axe as it crossed the edge of his peripheral vision, shouts, the explosive sounds of the Harley's exhaust system as he let the machine out, the chatter of subgunfire from ahead, Paul Rubenstein firing the Schmeisser into the air to hold them back.

Then Rourke was even with Rubenstein's bike, Rubenstein's machine charging ahead as well, the twin exhaust systems deafening in the clear, thin air.

Ahead the mountain seemed to evaporate, to drop away. "To the left—hurry!" It was Natalia shouting from behind him, Rourke twisting the Harley's fork, balancing it out with his combat-booted feet, wrenching the bike into a hard left, following along the edge of the flat expanse of rock. "Just ahead—a sharp right and you're clear of the mountain top, John!"

Rourke nodded, clamping the cigar tighter between his teeth, squinting despite the dark-lensed aviator-style sunglasses he wore, Natalia shouting loud now. "Twenty yards—then turn." Rourke slowed the Harley, then Natalia shouted, "Here! Here!"

Rourke wrenched the bike right, blind, not seeing the trail, but trusting Natalia as he had so many times before. The Harley lurched under him, bounced. Before them, running steeply downward but not so steeply as to be unnavigable, was a trail, the valley spreading out below.

Rourke slowed the bike again, balancing the machine with his feet as the trail dodged right then left then right. He glanced back once—Paul Rubenstein was coming along the trail and the cannibals were already gone from sight.

John Rourke remembered to breathe then.

Chapter Sixty-One

They had intercepted Michael and Madison in the valley, Natalia's route across the mountain and then down, despite a greater distance, faster than Michael's navigating the bike down the steeper trail by walking it.

They had ridden long into the night, the moon bright, traveling on until nearly dawn to be far gone from the Place and the ones Madison had called Them. A sparse meal—Madison had tried meat again and Michael had patiently explained to her that the meat of domestic animals or wild game was all right to eat. She had not eaten much, John Rourke had noticed.

They had slept a few hours, Rourke, his son and Paul Rubenstein each taking a two-hour shift on guard, then taking to the trail again without breakfast, by midmorning.

They settled into a schedule, reaching the Retreat the prime objective, stopping once to leave the route and locate one of the strategic fuel sites to gas up the Harleys and the spare gas canisters, then to move on.

John Rourke and his son had agreed—to return

to the wooded area where Michael had found the parachute, then to fan out and search for the wreckage of the aircraft to learn its source.

But after Christmas.

They had ridden hard through the day, and long into the night now, the Retreat so close and the date December twenty-fourth. Christmas—always a time Sarah had at once enjoyed and found somehow sad. John Rourke had no desire to make this Christmas sadder.

They had crossed the remains of a paved road and started up the long mountain road toward the main entrance of the Retreat, John Rourke rolling back the cuff of his bomber jacket to read the face of the Rolex—it was smudged with the light snow as soon as he rolled back the cuff and he wiped this away to better read the watch face. It was nearly midnight—and very soon, before it was actually Christmas morning, they would be "home". He felt a smile cross his lips. "Home," he murmured.

"John!"

It was Natalia's voice from behind him, muffled sounding, his back shielding her from the wind.

"What is it?" he said over his shoulder, slowing the Harley Low Rider under them.

"For a moment—stop and look up there."

Rourke slowed the Harley even more, making a wide arc with it, Michael with Madison behind him stopping just ahead of them, Paul stopping beside them. "We're almost home, Dad—what's up?"

Paul Rubenstein stopped beside them, laughing. "You didn't remember to wish me happy Hanukkah, but I'll wish you Merry Christmas anyway."

Rourke reached out and clasped his old friend on the back. "Happy Hanukkah then."

"You can remember me on May Day," Natalia laughed, "but look up there—all of you."

The snow was a shower, the sky surprisingly clear, a wide opening in the clouds to the east.

Light. One. Then another, then another, and still more, pinpoints, moving.

"The radio—we can signal them!" Michael shouted.

"Holy shit—the Eden Project, it's gotta be," Paul Rubenstein murmured.

"Yes." John Rourke nodded. "I doubt they'll be able to read our signal—but, maybe, we can try to—" But the clouds covered the opening in the sky now and the pinpoints of moving light were no longer visible. Had the atmosphere been the way it was when the Eden Project fleet had left the Earth five centuries earlier to travel in cryogenic sleep to the edge of the solar system and back, the shuttles would never have been visible at all, Rourke realized.

"They will find us—or we'll find them," Natalia said from behind him. It would be a long night, Rourke knew—listening for radio signals, alternately transmitting, observing in the cold from the top of the mountain to attempt to get a fix on the crafts if they passed overhead again. Coincidence or providence, Rourke wondered. He

233

dismissed the question.

Rourke twisted in the saddle to better see Natalia's face. He took her face in his hands, the wind catching at her hair, her cheeks cold to the touch, her lips drawing out into a smile. "Merry Christmas, John."

He smiled, wondering—but he drew her face toward him, kissing her lips, holding her there.

Chapter Sixty-Two

All was ready, his meager things prepared for the journey—an historic journey, he had told himself.

The old wounds bothered him not at all.

His speed with a gun was fast—very fast. Faster, he wondered? Faster than John Rourke?

The vial of the cryogenic serum he had paid so much to obtain when he had first learned of the Eden Project long before the Night of The War. The gunfight—he had lost.

But some few of his faithful—he would sing their names to the pages of history—they had taken him, found him the best of care in secret and when the inevitability of it had been known, helped him to survive.

He closed his eyes tightly, a pressure behind them he could feel, then opening them, staring at the sky—it was already Christmas. And the present he so much wanted to bestow—the gift of death—he could not yet give.

"Soon," he whispered to the morning stars, to the horizon beyond the mountain top where he had forged his plans, begun it all.

Footsteps crunched in the snow behind him and he turned around.

"All is ready. But there are strange signals coming over the radio—it is perhaps the time. The words are garbled—but I think they are English. It is a signal like none I have ever heard."

"The Eden Project. So much the better—so much the better."

"There is no way to be certain."

"I am certain. When the pain was all that consumed me, it seemed somehow to deepen my perception, to heighten my awareness—I could feel their presence before you spoke of it to me. We leave, then."

The other man, swathed in arctic parka and ski toque, raised his right hand in salute, "Yes, Comrade Colonel."

The snow through which he trod had been virgin until he had made his imprint on it, he thought as he walked, the subordinate following him. It would be that way with this new world as well.

THE WARLORD SERIES
by Jason Frost

THE WARLORD   (1189, $3.50)
A series of natural disasters, starting with an earthquake
and leading to nuclear power plant explosions, isolates
California. Now, cut off from any help, the survivors face
a world in which law is a memory and violence is the rule.

Only one man is fit to lead the people, a man raised among
Indians and trained by the Marines. He is Erik Raven-
smith, The Warlord—a deadly adversary and a hero for
our times.

#2: THE CUTTHROAT   (1308, $2.50)

#3: BADLAND   (1437, $2.50)

#4: PRISONLAND   (1506, $2.50)

#5: TERMINAL ISLAND   (1697, $2.50)